A Game of Chicken

They were securing the last post when the first shot came. The bullet struck the post between them, and they both leaped away. Clint drew his gun and came up onto one knee, looking for the source.

"Shootin' at you or me?" Locke the Widowmaker asked.

"Me, I think," Clint said. "Somebody's been taking potshots at me all month."

"Let's find out," Locke said, standing up.

"Locke, don't!"

Locke stood there, stock-still, waiting for the shot that didn't come.

"Looks like they don't want me," he said.

"Duck down," Clint said. "Let's see." Clint started to stand up. He hadn't even straightened when a second shot came. The bullet hit the ground in fr him, and again he ducked.

"Now all we need to knoey're missin' on purpose," I

"I'm not williint said.

"Well," Lock ry circling around and see w

"Some tracks h said, "but nothin' else. Small feet. Maybe a an."

"A woman!"

"Sure." Locke stood up. "Never occurred to you a woman might wanna kill you?"

"John," Clint said, "if women wanted to kill me, I'd be dead by now."

DON'T MISS THESE
ALL-ACTION WESTERN SERIES
FROM THE BERKLEY PUBLISHING GROUP

THE GUNSMITH by J. R. Roberts

Clint Adams was a legend among lawmen, outlaws, and ladies. They called him . . . the Gunsmith.

LONGARM by Tabor Evans

The popular long-running series about Deputy U.S. Marshal Custis Long—his life, his loves, his fight for justice.

SLOCUM by Jake Logan

Today's longest-running action Western. John Slocum rides a deadly trail of hot blood and cold steel.

BUSHWHACKERS by B. J. Lanagan

An action-packed series by the creators of Longarm! The rousing adventures of the most brutal gang of cutthroats ever assembled—Quantrill's Raiders.

DIAMONDBACK by Guy Brewer

Dex Yancey is Diamondback, a Southern gentleman turned con man when his brother cheats him out of the family fortune. Ladies love him. Gamblers hate him. But nobody pulls one over on Dex . . .

WILDGUN by Jack Hanson

The blazing adventures of mountain man Will Barlow—from the creators of Longarm!

TEXAS TRACKER by Tom Calhoun

J. T. Law: the most relentless—and dangerous—manhunter in all Texas. Where sheriffs and posses fail, he's the best man to bring in the most vicious outlaws—for a price.

THE GUNSMITH

323

A DAUGHTER'S REVENGE

J. R. ROBERTS

JOVE BOOKS, NEW YORK

THE BERKLEY PUBLISHING GROUP
Published by the Penguin Group
Penguin Group (USA) Inc.
375 Hudson Street, New York, New York 10014, USA

Penguin Group (Canada), 90 Eglinton Avenue East, Suite 700, Toronto, Ontario M4P 2Y3, Canada
(a division of Pearson Penguin Canada Inc.)
Penguin Books Ltd., 80 Strand, London WC2R 0RL, England
Penguin Group Ireland, 25 St. Stephen's Green, Dublin 2, Ireland (a division of Penguin Books Ltd.)
Penguin Group (Australia), 250 Camberwell Road, Camberwell, Victoria 3124, Australia
(a division of Pearson Australia Group Pty. Ltd.)
Penguin Books India Pvt. Ltd., 11 Community Centre, Panchsheel Park, New Delhi—110 017, India
Penguin Group (NZ), 67 Apollo Drive, Rosedale, North Shore 0632, New Zealand
(a division of Pearson New Zealand Ltd.)
Penguin Books (South Africa) (Pty.) Ltd., 24 Sturdee Avenue, Rosebank, Johannesburg 2196,
South Africa

Penguin Books Ltd., Registered Offices: 80 Strand, London WC2R 0RL, England

This is a work of fiction. Names, characters, places, and incidents either are the product of the author's imagination or are used fictitiously, and any resemblance to actual persons, living or dead, business establishments, events, or locales is entirely coincidental.

A DAUGHTER'S REVENGE

A Jove Book / published by arrangement with the author

PRINTING HISTORY
Jove edition / November 2008

ISBN: 978-0-515-14547-2

JOVE®
Jove Books are published by The Berkley Publishing Group,
a division of Penguin Group (USA) Inc.,
375 Hudson Street, New York, New York 10014.
JOVE® is a registered trademark of Penguin Group (USA) Inc.
The "J" design is a trademark belonging to Penguin Group (USA) Inc.

PRINTED IN THE UNITED STATES OF AMERICA

10 9 8 7 6 5 4 3 2 1

ONE

A couple more chunks of hot lead chipped away from the boulder Clint was using for cover. In the distance he could see Eclipse, who was far enough away to be safe from any flying lead or rock. But that also meant that his rifle was far away from him, too.

He had his pistol in his hand, but it wasn't going to do him much good. The shooter was a good distance off himself, and was taking potshots at Clint with a rifle. Clint finally holstered his gun, for all the good it was doing him.

They were at an impasse, unless one of them decided to move. He was safe behind his boulder; the shooter was safe because he was too far away to be threatened by Clint's handgun.

Wondering who was shooting at him was a futile endeavor. This had happened so often he'd stopped taking it personally. This was about the Gunsmith, not Clint Adams.

There were two kinds of men who tried to kill the Gunsmith. First was this kind of coward, who tried to bushwhack him while hiding, just so he could say he killed the Gunsmith.

The second type of man came at him with more honor and integrity, although the goal was the same: to kill the Gunsmith. But at least they came right at him and faced him head-on, matching their own skill with a gun against his. He had much more respect for them, even when they came at him with help. It was the bushwhackers and backshooters he had no use for. He would rather face three men in the street than one bushwhacker from behind a rock or a tree.

Clint surveyed the surrounding area. This was Arizona, and the ground around him was flat and hard. He was lucky to have found this boulder to use for cover.

He closed his eyes and searched back into his memory. He only needed to recall what he had seen minutes ago. Flat on his right, but a rise on his left, topped by a couple of dead trees. That had to be where the shooter was.

There was no cover that he could use to work his way around behind the shooter. He was stuck, and while the shooter probably had his horse nearby, along with a canteen of water, Clint had nothing. If they played a long waiting game, Clint was going to lose.

He could afford to wait a couple of hours, see if the shooter became impatient, but after that he was going to have to make some kind of move.

But for now he sat with his back to the boulder and waited.

Up on the hill, behind the dead cottonwoods, the shooter sighted down the barrel of his rifle, waiting for Clint Adams to poke his head—or any other part of his body—out from behind the rock.

Unlike most bushwhackers, this one had more in mind than just killing the Gunsmith for the credit it would bring him. No, this particular shooter had vengeance in mind, and for vengeance he could be patient and wait a long time.

This had been ten years in coming, so a few more hours would not make a difference.

Two hours later Clint swiped at a drop of perspiration that had been about to drip from the tip of his nose. It was midday, and hot. That, too, would work in favor of the shooter, for even a dead cottonwood could offer shade from the sun.

Clint sat forward far enough to be able to see Eclipse. The big Darley Arabian was fairly safe, though not out of range. If the shooter decided to, he could take the stallion down and leave Clint afoot. Clint wondered if he could convince Eclipse to move a little farther away.

He knew he could bring the horse to him at a gallop with a whistle if he wanted to, but that would put the animal in danger. Taking a run for the horse himself would test the marksmanship of the shooter, who'd had a clear first shot at him and missed. How would he fare with a quick-moving target?

Clint took off his hat and held it up above the boulder. Immediately, there was a shot that missed the hat but struck the rock. He wasn't dealing with an expert marksman. At least he had that in his favor.

He decided his best bet was to make a run for his

horse. His legs were stiff from sitting so long, so he began to flex and stretch them. He'd throw a couple of quick shots in the direction of the shooter, just in the hope of making him flinch. Once he was in the saddle, he had the option of riding off out of range and then circling back to see if he could get a jump on the shooter. Or he could just keep going and forget the incident. Chalk it up to somebody who saw an opportunity and missed. If the shooter followed him and tried again, he could deal with it then.

On the other hand, why let somebody try to bushwhack him and not make him pay for it?

He moved up into a crouch and drew his gun. Hopefully, Eclipse would see him coming and stand still. If the horse started toward him, it would cut down the distance he had to cover but also bring the animal farther into range of the shooter.

Okay, he was ready to make his run. Catching the shooter unaware would also increase his chances of making it. Everything had to go just right in order for him to make it.

He braced himself, and then sprang.

TWO

One month later

Clint held the fence post in place while his friend John Locke filled in the hole, securing the post in the ground.

"Only four more," Locke said, standing back.

"That all?" Clint asked, brushing off his hands and then wiping the sweat from his brow with his sleeve.

"Hey," Locke said, grabbing a canteen from the nearby buckboard, "you volunteered, remember?"

"I remember asking if there was anything I could help with," Clint said. "I didn't think you'd have me sinking fence posts."

"You know," Locke said, handing over the canteen, "those dime novelists from New York would love this."

"I know," Clint said. "I can just see the title now. *The Gunsmith and the Widowmaker Sink Fence Posts.*"

"Big seller," Locke said.

Clint drank some water and handed the canteen back.

"This is a nice spread you've got here, John," he said, turning serious.

"My chance to be a legitimate rancher," Locke said.

Locke had been many things—lawman, bounty hunter, some even said an outlaw. The one thing Clint never thought he'd see was John Locke become a rancher.

"Is that what you really want?"

Locke took off his hat, wiped his head with a neckerchief.

"I'm a little older than you, Clint," Locke said. "I'm tired of ridin' around the country with a gun. Time for me to settle down."

"Settling down usually involves a woman, John," Clint said. "You got one in mind?"

"No," Locke said, "nobody special, but that could come later. I don't mind bein' alone, though. That's not somethin' that bothers me."

"Well," Clint said, "I wish you luck, John. I don't know that I could settle down, myself. Not after all this time."

"You're welcome here anytime," Locke said. "Especially after you help me sink the rest of these fence posts."

"That's the price, huh?"

"Like I said," Locke replied, spreading his arms, "only four more."

"Okay, then," Clint said, "let's get it done."

They went to the buckboard, pulled off another post.

They were securing the last post when the first shot came. The bullet struck the post between them, and they both leaped away.

Locke's gun was on the buckboard, but Clint's gun was at his waist. He drew it and came up onto one knee, looking for the source of the shot.

Locke rolled toward the buckboard, snatched his gun from its holster, and came up to one knee.

"See anythin'?" Locke asked, scanning the countryside.

"No."

"Shootin' at you or me?" Locke the Widowmaker asked.

"Me, I think," Clint said. "Somebody's been taking potshots at me all month."

"That one came pretty close."

"I know," Clint said. "Makes me wonder if they've been missing on purpose."

"Let's find out," Locke said.

"How?"

"Like this."

He stood up, his hands down at his sides.

"Locke, don't!"

Locke stood there, stock-still, waiting for the shot that didn't come.

"Looks like they don't want me," he said. "Unless they're gone."

"Okay, duck down," Clint said. "Let's see."

Locke crouched down behind the buckboard and

Clint started to stand up. He hadn't even straightened when a second shot came. The bullet hit the ground in front of him, and he ducked back down again.

"Okay," he said, "so they're after me."

"Now all we need to know is whether or not they're missin' on purpose," Locke said.

"I'm not willing to stand up straight to find that out," Clint said.

"Well, what do you want to do?"

"Well, in the past they usually would just quit and go away, and wait to try some other time," Clint said. "One time I made a run for my horse and got away."

"Did you circle back?"

"No," Clint said. "I didn't think it was worth it."

"Well," Locke said, "maybe we should try circling around and see what we can find out."

"I suppose so."

Locke looked over at him.

"You that used to bein' shot at?"

"Aren't you?"

"Not anymore."

THREE

Clint had left Eclipse back at John Locke's place, and both men had ridden out on the buckboard. If they were going to circle around on this shooter, they were going to have to do it on foot.

"You go left, I'll go right," Clint said.

"Just say go," Locke said.

Clint took a deep breath, then said, "Okay . . . go!"

They each took off running, which did not bring any shots. They used various forms of cover—trees, brush, rocks—to work their way around. They didn't know where the shooter was, but they were able to figure out where he had to have been.

Clint arrived at the spot just a split second after Locke.

"Some tracks here," Locke said, "but nothin' else."

Clint let Locke crouch down to check the tracks. He was, after all, the better tracker of the two.

"Small feet," Locke said. "A small man, or maybe a woman."

"A woman!"

"Sure." Locke stood up. "Never occurred to you a woman might wanna kill you?"

"John," Clint said, "if women wanted to kill me, I'd be dead by now."

Locke chuckled.

"Me, too, I guess."

They looked around and Locke found the sign of a horse.

"Same thing here," he said. "Small animal. Rode off south."

Clint stared off into the distance.

"You wanna track her?" Locke asked.

"I could, I guess."

"Only if you want to ask her why she's tryin' to kill you," Locke said. "I could ride along with you—"

"No, no," Clint said, staring down at the ground, "that's not necessary. I can follow this trail pretty well."

Locke looked up.

"There's no rain in the offing," he said. "You can wait until mornin'—although we're pretty much done with the fence posts. You could leave now, if you want."

"No," Clint said. "I was planning on moving on in the morning, anyway. I might as well stick to my plan."

"Let's get back to the house, then," Locke said. "I've got a couple of steaks waitin' for us."

"Sounds good," Clint said.

They walked back to the buckboard, loaded up their supplies, and rode back to the house.

"You're a good cook, John," Clint said after their meal. "You'll make some gal a fine husband someday."

"I get a wife, I'm not gonna be doin' the cookin'," Locke said. "I can tell ya that. Let's go outside."

They went out onto the porch of the small two-room house Locke had built with his own hands. He gave Clint a cigar and then he told of his plans to add rooms on, maybe even a second floor, eventually.

"I'll get me some hands eventually, too," he said.

"What are you going to raise?"

"Horses," Locke said. "I know horses pretty well."

"Cattle's a lucrative business."

"I don't know shit about cattle," Locke said. "Horses I know. Like that animal of yours. Too bad he's a gelding or I could breed him."

"Sorry, gelding him wasn't my decision. That was decided by P. T. Barnum."

"So you said," Locke replied. "Tell me a bit about meeting Barnum. Was he as big a liar as everybody says he was?"

"Well," Clint said, "I wouldn't exactly call it lying . . ."

They talked awhile longer, working on a bottle of whiskey until it was empty, but oddly neither of them was drunk.

"You sure you don't want me to ride awhile with you tomorrow?" Locke asked. "I've got to go into Las Vegas anyway for some supplies."

"You'll need to take your buckboard, then," Clint said. "Besides, the trail leads in the opposite direction."

"So, how many times you figure this same person has taken a shot at you?"

"I didn't think it was the same person at first," Clint said, "but then I started thinking about it."

"They always miss?"

"Always."

"Sounds like maybe they've been tryin' to get your attention."

"Well, they did it," Clint said. "When that bullet smacked into the fence post between us, it was the closest they've come."

"Well," Locke said, "I guess we better get a good night's sleep then. You can bunk out here on the porch if you want, or inside on the floor. Your choice."

"I'll take the floor," Clint said.

In the morning they had some coffee and then Locke hitched his horse to the buckboard while Clint saddled Eclipse.

They walked their animals out of Locke's barn and the big man stuck his hand out.

"It was good to see you, Clint," he said. "Thanks for stoppin' by—and thanks for the help with the fence posts. You ever want to do a few more days' work, you let me know."

"This kind of work is too hard, John," Clint said. "Mark my words, you'll be back in the saddle soon."

"Think so?" Locke laughed and shook his head. "We'll see."

The two men shook hands again. Locke climbed aboard his buckboard and headed for Las Vegas, New Mexico, while Clint turned Eclipse south.

FOUR

Clint followed the trail for three days. Eventually, it petered out somewhere just over the border in Colorado. John Locke probably could have picked it up again, but Clint couldn't. He decided to forget about it. If, as he and Locke had surmised, somebody was trying to get his attention, they'd keep trying.

He turned Eclipse and headed for Denver.

The second night in Denver Clint had supper with his friend Talbot Roper, who was the best private detective in the country.

"Saw John Locke a few days ago," Clint said.

"What's the Widowmaker doing?" Roper asked.

"Raising horses."

"You're kidding."

"No."

"Where?"

"Near Las Vegas, New Mexico."

"How long do you think that will last?" Roper asked, sawing a piece off his steak.

"Doesn't matter how long you or I think it's going to last," Clint said. "It only matters what he thinks."

"And what does he think?" Roper asked. "Or what does he *think* he thinks?"

"He thinks he's going to put down his gun, put away his saddle, and raise horses."

"He can't do that any more than you or I can," Roper said. "He should know that."

"Maybe he does."

They talked for another couple of hours, trading war stories and talking about things that had happened since they'd last seen each other.

Roper paid the check—he was the host—and then they walked outside. Almost immediately the shot came. A bullet gouged out a piece of the wall next to the door. Roper hit the ground, but Clint stood his ground.

"Are you crazy?" Roper demanded. "Get down!"

"Don't worry," Clint said. "They're not shooting at you."

"At you?"

"Not really at me, either," Clint said. He was studying the windows and doorways across the way.

"I don't get it."

"See? No second shot. Come on, get up."

Carefully, Roper got to his feet. When there was no shot, he relaxed.

"Want to tell me what's goin' on?" he asked.

"Somebody's been trying to get my attention for about a month."

"By shooting at you?"

"And missing."

"Why don't they just come up to you and talk to you?" Roper asked.

"I don't know," Clint said. "I've cut a trail once or twice, but lost it. I guess I'm just waiting for whoever it is to get up the nerve to approach me."

"You want to go across the street and take a look?" the detective asked.

"No, forget it," Clint said. "You headed home?"

Roper shook his head.

"I've got to meet a client."

"This late?"

"Clients come in all shapes and sizes, Clint, and at all hours. Stayin' in town long?"

"Probably leaving tomorrow."

Roper extended his hand.

"It was good to see you," Roper said. "Give me some warning next time and plan to stay a little longer."

"I'll do it, Tal. See you."

Roper waved and walked off, still not convinced there wouldn't be another shot.

FIVE

Clint went back to his hotel, the Denver House, which was where he always stayed when he came to town. Given the fact that this was general knowledge, remarkably few shots had been taken at him when he was there.

"Mr. Adams?" the desk clerk called as Clint walked by on his way to the staircase.

Clint detoured over to the desk.

"There's a woman waiting for you in the bar, sir," the young clerk said.

"A woman? Did she leave a name?"

"No, sir," the clerk said. "She just asked me to give you that message."

"A woman," Clint repeated. "Young, old, fat, skinny?"

"Not old, perhaps in her early thirties," the clerk said. "Dark-haired, very attractive, well dressed. I suggested that the bar might not be the best place for her to wait, but she wouldn't hear of it. She said she needed a drink."

"All right, thanks," Clint said. "I'll go and check it out for myself."

Clint walked over to the entrance to the bar and stopped just inside. The bar's regular clientele was usually made up of guests, and businessmen from the area. It was evening, so there were quite a few men there having after-supper drinks, or late business meetings. Among them, sitting alone at a table, was the woman the clerk had described. Raven-haired and lovely, she sat alone, nursing what appeared to be a glass of brandy. Next to the brandy snifter was an empty shot glass. Apparently, she'd had that drink she needed.

Clint walked over and presented himself at her table.

"Excuse me. I understand you're waiting for me?" he asked.

"I am if you're Clint Adams," she said.

"I am."

"Then sit, please," she said. "Can I get you a drink?"

"Why don't I just go to the bar and get one," he said, "and another for you."

"No," she said. "I'll just finish this one. Thank you."

"I'll be right back."

He went to the bar for a beer.

"You must have some line, friend," the bartender said.

"Why's that?"

"She's already turned away five men who tried." The bartender set a cold beer down in front of him.

"It's all in the wrist," Clint said, and carried his beer back to the table.

"You have me at a disadvantage," he said as he sat

across from her. "You know my name, but I don't know yours."

"My name is Rose Kellogg," she said. "Does that name mean anything to you?"

He sat back and stared at her. Was he supposed to know her? He'd been with a lot of women over the years, but he usually remembered.

"I'm afraid it doesn't," he admitted.

"What about Tom Kellogg?" she asked. "Does that name mean anything?"

Now he sat back, stunned. He hadn't heard that name in almost . . . what? Twenty years?

"Ah," she said. "I see that it does."

"Yes."

"He was my father."

Clint didn't know what to say. He was sorry. Would that carry any weight?

"Look," Rose said, "I don't know if you really killed my father or not, and I'm not here to ask you that question."

"Why are you here, then?"

"I have a younger sister," Rose said. "Her name is Laura. I'm afraid that she is totally convinced that you killed our father all those years ago."

"I see."

"And I'm afraid she might try to kill you at some point."

"Do you mean she might try it herself, or have someone do it for her?"

"I'm afraid she might do it herself," Rose said. "You see, we live back East now, in Philadelphia. My mother took us away from the West after my father died. Recently, Laura left home, and she took a rifle with her."

"And you think she might have come West to try to kill me?"

"Yes."

"Well . . ."

"Has she?" Rose asked. "You didn't—"

"What? Kill her? No, Miss Kellogg, I haven't killed your sister," he said, "but somebody's been taking shots at me for the past month wherever I go."

"Have you ever seen who it is?"

"No, but according to the tracks they've been leaving behind it's somebody small, like a woman. Is your sister a small person?"

"About average for a woman, I guess."

"Smaller than you?"

"Yes," she said. "I'm five foot eight. Laura is smaller and lighter than me."

"Can she handle a gun?"

"Very well."

"A handgun, or a rifle?"

"She can shoot with a rifle very accurately," Rose said. "I don't believe she has any skill with a pistol."

"So tell me this, Miss Kellogg. If this is your sister who's been shooting at me, why has she been missing?"

"Every time?"

"Every time," he said. "Closer each time, but still a miss."

"I can only think of one reason," Rose said.

"And what's that?"

"She's been missing on purpose," Rose said. "She must not be ready to kill you . . . yet."

SIX

"The first thing I want to tell you," Clint said to Rose Kellogg, "is that I didn't kill your father."

"That doesn't matter to me," Rose said. "It's been years. My only concern is my sister. I don't want her to kill you, and I don't want you to kill her."

"What do you want me to do?" Clint asked.

"I want you to find her, and stop her," Rose said. "I want you to take the rifle away from her, and send her home."

"You need a detective for that, Miss Kellogg," Clint said. "As it happens, the best detective in the country lives right here in Denver, and is a friend of mine."

She sat forward and leaned on the table.

"I don't care how you do it," she said. "Use your detective friend, if you like. But I want you to be the one who finds her and stops her."

"Why me?"

"If you're telling the truth about not killing my father, she needs to hear that," she said. "You need to convince her of that so she'll give up this idea of killing you."

"How old is your sister, Miss Kellogg?"

"She's twenty-two."

"So she's an adult," Clint said. "You should be able to reason with her."

"She was two when our father was killed," Rose said. "She's been told since that time that you killed him."

"Who told her that?"

"My mother," Rose said. "She told Laura that every day of her life until she died when Laura was eighteen."

"And since then you've been telling her I didn't kill him?"

"I didn't know that, did I?" she asked. "How could I tell her that? No, I've been telling her that killing you won't bring our father back."

"And?"

"And she's convinced she can't go on with her life until she's killed you."

"But you do believe that I didn't kill him, right?" Clint asked.

She stood up.

"I don't have to believe that, Mr. Adams," she said.

"But I told you—"

"And I told you it didn't matter at this point," she said. "Just find her and convince her."

"Do you know where she is?"

"No."

"But you knew she took a shot at me tonight? About an hour ago?"

She sat back down heavily.

"No, I didn't know that. Then she's in Denver."

"Apparently," Clint said. "The question is, how did she know I was? And how did you know I was?"

"She's been sending me telegrams," she said. "Here," she said, producing them from her bag.

Clint read them. They were each postmarked somewhere he'd been. He looked at the dates. He couldn't be sure, but . . .

"I believe all these telegrams were sent either just before or just after she took a shot at me," he told her, handing them back.

"But the Denver one is dated three days ago," she said.

"Yes," Clint said, "that's a break in the pattern. Or . . ."

"Or what?"

"Or maybe she wanted to give you time to get here?" he said. "Did you come here from Philadelphia?"

"No," she said. "I was in Chicago when I got it. I was already on my way west to try to find her."

"Miss Kellogg," he said, "can you explain to me how your sister has managed to find me each time? And take a shot at me without me knowing she was there?"

"No, I can't," she said. "Perhaps you are becoming careless as you become . . . older?"

That stung, but he didn't let it show.

"No, that can't be it."

"Why not?"

"Because the minute I become careless," he said, "I'll be dead the next."

This time when she got up she appeared determined to leave.

"Just find her," she said. "And don't kill her."

"And where will you be, Miss Kellogg?"

"I'm staying here, Mr. Adams," she said, "and I'll be here until I've heard that you've found her."

"And if she's left Denver and I have to track her?" he asked.

"It wont matter," she said. "I'll still be here. I won't be leaving until you find her."

"Miss Kellogg," he said, "about your father—"

She turned and walked out of the bar without another word.

SEVEN

Clint remained in the bar long enough to have another beer. It bothered him that a twenty-two-year-old girl may have been trying to kill him this past month—or was planning to kill him after playing with him—because she thought he'd killed her father twenty years ago. And what about Rose Kellogg? What did she believe? In spite of her protestations, Clint did not believe for a minute that it didn't matter to her whether or not he'd killed her father. He assumed she was putting that in the back of her mind until she solved the more pressing matter of saving her sister from becoming a killer—or saving her life.

While Clint had no intention of killing the girl, it was sometimes very difficult not to kill someone who was trying to kill you.

He checked the time. It was too late to get ahold of Tal Roper, and besides, he didn't know where the detective was meeting with his client. He'd have to wait until morning to "rope" his friend into this mess—no pun intended.

He finished his beer and went up to his room.

Dirk Wilson looked up as the door opened and Laura Kellogg walked in carrying her rifle.

"I'm surprised the police didn't pick you up for walkin' down the street with that."

"I was careful."

"Did you kill him?"

"No," she said, putting the rifle down in the corner. "I didn't."

"Good."

She gave the man a hard look.

"I could have, you know," she said. "I wanted to."

"I told you, Laura," Wilson said, "this is the best way. This will drive him crazy, and make him easy pickin's later."

"He was easy pickings several times over already," she complained, sitting down on the bed next to him.

"Don't worry," he said, putting his arm around her, "you'll get your chance."

She shrugged off his arm and said, "I told you not to do that."

"I know," he said. "I heard you all hundred times. I'm just waitin' for you to change your mind."

"Well, you'll have to wait a long time," she said.

"There's somethin' you should know."

"What's that?"

"Your sister's in Denver."

"Rose? What's she doing here?"

"Lookin' for you."

"Where is she?"

"The Denver House."

Laura stood up, shouting, "That's where Adams is staying!"

"I know."

"Is she here to kill him?"

"More likely to warn him."

"No," Laura said, shaking her head, "she wouldn't."

"Maybe, maybe not."

Laura started for the door.

"Where are you goin'?" he asked.

"I've got to talk to her."

Wilson rushed to get between her and the door.

"That's not a good idea."

"Why not?"

"Like you said, Adams is stayin' there."

"He doesn't know what I look like," she said. "He doesn't even know it's been me shooting at him all this time."

"And that's because I been findin' him for you," Wilson pointed out. "But what if your sister did talk with him? And told him about you? And what you look like?"

"I told you, she wouldn't."

"Didn't you tell me she didn't want you to kill him?" he asked.

"Yes, but—"

"Then maybe this is her way of tryin' to stop ya," Wilson said.

"Dirk . . . What do I do?"

"What you been doin'," he said. "Just do like I tell

ya. This is the West, girl. Don't nobody know how things are done out here better than me."

"So, what do we do?"

"Get a good night's rest," Wilson said, "and tomorrow if ya still wanna talk to your sister, I'll go and talk to her. I'll set it up."

Laura thought a moment, then said, "All right, yes. That does sound better."

"Sure it is," Wilson said. "You hungry? There's a place around the corner that's pretty good, and hardly anybody goes there."

"I could eat something . . ."

"Sure you could," he said, "and then a good night's rest. Whataya say?"

She smiled wanly and said, "Well, all right. You haven't steered me wrong so far."

"No, I haven't," he said, "and I won't."

Not until I'm good and ready, he added to himself.

EIGHT

Clint woke the next morning to the realization that a twenty-two-year-old girl he'd never met wanted to kill him.

Okay, he'd known that when he went to sleep, but suddenly he "realized" it.

It was not a good feeling.

He went downstairs, had a breakfast he barely tasted—which annoyed him, because he usually loved his breakfasts in Denver—and then caught a cab in front of the hotel to Talbot Roper's office.

"Can I help you?"

The woman sitting at the desk in the outer office was not the type who usually occupied that place. She was new, and they had never seen each other before. She was in her forties, not her twenties, and was handsome rather than pretty or beautiful. In fact, she exhibited more class than the women who usually sat in that seat.

"Good morning," he said. "My name is Clint Adams. I'm a friend of Tal's and—"

"Oh, yes," she said. "He's mentioned you many times. Shall I tell him you're here?"

"Please."

She stood up, walked to Roper's door, knocked, and entered. Clint liked the way she moved. After a few seconds she returned to the doorway, left the door open.

"You can go in, sir."

"Thank you . . ."

"Melanie."

"Thank you, Melanie, and since we'll be seeing more of each other while I'm here, why don't you just call me Clint?"

"All right, Clint."

He entered and she graced him with a smile before closing the door behind him.

"You're impossible," Roper said from behind his desk.

"Why?"

"I finally hire a mature secretary, and you're flirting with her."

"What's wrong with mature women?"

"Nothing."

"I'm surprised you've switched."

"I'm gettin' older," Roper said, "and I don't need the constant distraction around the office."

"She's not a distraction?"

"I didn't think she'd be," Roper said. "What can I do for you?"

Clint sat down in the visitor's chair and regarded his friend across his huge desk.

"That shot that was taken at me last night?"

"Yup."

"Turns out it was taken by the same person who's been shooting at me for weeks," Clint said.

"And now you know who it is?"

"Yes, a twenty-two-year-old young woman named Laura Kellogg."

"Kellogg?" Roper frowned. "As in . . ."

"Tom Kellogg, right."

"And she's . . ."

"His daughter," Clint said. "She was two when he . . . died, and her mother has convinced her over the years that I killed him."

"And you know this how?"

"I got a visit last night from her older sister, Rose," Clint said. "Told me the whole story."

"And the older sister doesn't think you killed their father?"

"I don't know about that," Clint said. "I told her I didn't, but she doesn't want to deal with that right now. She wants to keep her sister from killing me, or me from killing her sister."

"You don't intend—"

"Of course not."

"But it's kind of hard—"

"I know."

Roper glared at Clint. "You gonna let me finish a sentence?"

There was a knock at that point and Melanie entered with two cups of coffee.

"Thought you gentlemen might like some of this," she said.

It smelled strong, the way Clint liked it, and it was black for both of them.

"Thanks, Mel," Roper said.

She smiled and left.

"Mel?" Clint said.

"Her idea."

"Melanie is such a pretty name . . ."

"Like I said, it was her idea."

"And she calls you . . ."

"Boss."

"Well, Boss, you think you can help me?"

"If she's still in Denver, we can probably locate her," Roper said. He pulled over a pad of paper and picked up a pencil. "Tell me everything you know . . ."

NINE

As Clint left Roper's office, Melanie turned and smiled at him. That was all the encouragement he needed.

"So, are you from Denver?" he asked.

"Born and raised," she said.

"That means you know where all the best restaurants are, right?"

"From what I hear," she said, "you come here fairly often. Seems to me you'd know where you like to eat."

"Yeah, but nobody knows the good restaurants like a native."

"Is this your cute way of asking me to dine with you tonight?"

"Cute? I didn't think it was cute—"

"Because if it is," she said, cutting him off, "maybe you should just ask."

"Okay," he said. "Melanie, would you like to dine with me tonight?"

"I'd love to."

"Oh," he said, "I should tell you that a time or two lately I've been known to have been shot at."

"How exciting," she said. "I'm sure everyone at Le Steak will be excited, too."

"Is that where we'll be going?"

"It's a terrible name, but it has the best steaks in Denver."

"Sounds good, then. Shall I pick you up—"

"Why don't I come to your hotel?" she said. "Where are you staying?"

"The Denver House."

"Ah, you go first-class, don't you?"

"I've been staying there for years, since before it was a first-class hotel."

"Well, I'll meet you in the lobby at—what? Six?"

"Six sounds good."

"And thank you for the invitation."

"Thank you for accepting." He moved closer to the desk. "There's just one thing."

"What's that?"

"Maybe we shouldn't mention this to Roper just yet," he suggested.

"There's nothing going on between Mr. Roper and me," she assured him.

"Just the same," he said, "I'd like to keep this between you and me."

"All right."

"I'll see you at six."

Dirk Wilson waited outside the Denver House hotel for Rose Kellogg to appear. When she did, he wasted no time confronting her.

"Excuse me, Miss Kellogg?"

She stopped short and looked him up and down.

"Yes?"

"Miss Rose Kellogg?" he asked. "Your sister is Laura Kellogg?"

"That's right," she said. "Do you know Laura?"

"I know that she's in trouble, ma'am," he said. "She sent me to get you, fetch you to her."

"Where is she? Is she all right?"

"She's fine, ma'am . . . for now. But she really needs to see you."

"Of course," Rose said. "Take me to her."

"That's why I'm here, ma'am," Wilson said. "Will you come with me, please?"

"Of course," she said. "Which way?"

Clint left Roper's office and caught a cab back to the Denver House hotel. When he got there, he checked at the desk to see if Rose Kellogg was actually registered there. It was something he should have done the night before.

"Yes, sir. Miss Kellogg is registered," the clerk said.

"Do you know if she's in her room?"

"I haven't seen her leave, sir," the man said. "That's the best I can do."

"And can you tell me if she's had any guests?" Clint asked.

"Not while I've been on duty, sir."

"And how long is that?"

"Truthfully, sir, I've just come on duty."

"Okay, thanks."

"Yes, sir."

Clint went to the bar for an early beer. The place wasn't busy, as the businessmen were still in their offices and guests were either still in their rooms or out looking over the town. He ordered a beer and drank it standing at the bar.

TEN

Clint's window looked out over the front of the hotel. He'd gone back to his room after his beer and was standing at the window, his eyes flicking from window to window, door to door across the street. He was trying to figure out where the shot might have come from. He could have crossed over and checked out the rooftops, but in the end he decided it wouldn't do any good. The most he'd find might be a spent shell, and there was nothing he could do with that.

He was contemplating a late lunch, decided it would interfere with his supper with Melanie, when there was a knock on the door. He opened it with his gun still strapped to his hip. The uniformed policeman standing there looked right at the gun before he looked at Clint's face.

"Clint Adams?"

"That's right."

"Would you come with me, please?"

"Why?"

"My sergeant would like to talk to you."

"About what?"

"I can't say, sir," the man said. "But I was told if you refused I was to use force."

Now Clint looked the man up and down. *Beefy* was the first word that came to mind, heavy through the chest and shoulders, straining the seams on his uniform. Short of using his gun, Clint didn't know if he'd be able to resist if the man tried to use force.

"There won't be any need for force, Officer," Clint said. "I'll be happy to help, if I can . . . with whatever it is."

"Thank you, sir. This way?"

"After you," Clint said. "I'll lock my door and follow."

The man hesitated, then said, "Very good, sir."

When they got to the lobby, Clint was surprised when, instead of heading out the front door, the policeman took him the back way. When they got outside, Clint found more uniformed officers waiting in an area that was obviously used for garbage. One of the officers had three stripes on his arm.

"Here he is, Sarge."

"Any trouble, Davis?"

"No trouble," Davis said. "He came easy."

"What's this about, Sergeant?" Clint asked.

"Come with me, sir."

"Where now?"

"Just a few feet, sir," the sergeant said, "if you will?"

The sergeant took Clint over behind a pile of garbage that stank of rotten food. There Clint found himself looking at the body of a woman.

"Do you know her, sir?"

"I don't know," Clint said. "I can't see her face."

"Davis!"

Officer Davis came over, slid in behind the garbage, and gently turned the woman over. He had to brush some rotten lettuce from her face before Clint could see that it was Rose Kellogg.

"Yes, I know her."

"How, sir?"

"She's a guest in the hotel."

"That's all?"

Clint thought fast. Did he want to tell these nice officers that Rose's sister, Laura, apparently meant to kill him?

"We met yesterday for the first time," Clint said. "Had a drink together in the bar."

"And what did you talk about?"

"You know," Clint said, "getting acquainted, the things you talk about when you first meet somebody."

"I see. And can you explain why she had a slip of paper on her with your name and the name of this hotel on it?"

"I don't know," Clint said. "Maybe she wrote it down after we met so she wouldn't forget."

"Or maybe she wrote it down before she got here," the sergeant said. "Maybe she was here lookin' for you?"

"I don't know, Sergeant," Clint said. "She didn't say she was."

"All right, sir," the sergeant said. "Davis."

Davis let the woman roll over facedown again.

"How was she killed?" Clint asked.

"Looks like she was strangled, sir," Davis said. That drew him a hard stare from the sergeant, and he didn't say any more.

"Not plannin' to leave town anytime soon, are ya, sir?"

"No."

"Good. I'm sure the detectives will be wantin' to talk to you."

"What's your name, Sergeant?"

"O'Malley, sir. You can go."

Clint was staring down at Rose Kellogg, wondering what the woman had gotten herself into.

"Sir?"

"Oh," Clint said, "sorry. It's too bad. She seemed like a nice woman."

"Somebody didn't think so," the sergeant said.

ELEVEN

Clint went to the bar and sat nursing a beer where he and Rose had sat the day before. His mind was racing. If one of the Kellogg girls was going to get killed, he would have bet on Laura. Now that Rose was dead, he was confused. Did her death have anything to do with him? Or was it a coincidence? He should have asked the police if she had been robbed.

With Rose Kellogg dead he had no connection to Laura—if Rose had even known where her sister was. Clint wasn't convinced she had, but it didn't matter now that she was dead.

His only chance now was that Roper could locate Laura Kellogg. But what was he going to do until then?

He finished his beer and went back to the lobby. The same clerk was on duty, but Clint decided he needed to talk with the night clerk. Maybe he saw something. Maybe somebody had been asking about Rose before this clerk came on.

"That would be Jed, sir," the clerk said. "He comes back at four."

"Do you know where he lives? Can you give me his address?"

"I couldn't do that," the man said. "You could talk to the manager, but by the time you convinced him, and found Jed's place . . ."

"I might as well wait until four."

"Yes, sir."

"Okay, thanks."

"Sir?"

"Yes?"

"The police . . ."

"You'll be hearing about it soon enough," Clint told him.

"Yes, sir."

Clint checked the time. The clerk would be coming on duty in two hours. He hated to just sit around all that time and do nothing, but he didn't have much of a choice. He decided to go ahead and get himself a small snack that wouldn't interfere with his supper with Melanie.

He left the hotel, walked down the block to a small café, and killed the entire two hours there.

He was waiting in the lobby when Melanie arrived, which she misinterpreted.

"You're eager," she said.

She looked lovely, wearing an off-the-shoulder blue dress covered by a shawl. Her auburn hair was shiny and worn long, past her shoulders, where in the office she had worn it up.

"I hate to disappoint you," he said, "but I was eager to find out if Roper was in his office when you left."

"No," she said. "I locked up when I left. Why? Has something happened?"

"Well, nothing that I want to ruin your meal with," he said.

"Nonsense," she said. "I've worked for Roper long enough to know that things happen when you least expect them."

"Well," he said, "I think this qualifies."

She put her hand on his arm and said, "Let's go on to the restaurant and you can tell me there. You might as well have a nice meal at the same time."

"You're a gem," he said.

She smiled and said, "I know."

TWELVE

Over a delicious dinner Clint told Melanie about Rose and Laura Kellogg, and the events of the afternoon.

"My God, that's awful," she said. "First, to find out that a young girl wants to kill you, then to be asked for help by her sister, only to have her killed. Do you think—" She stopped short.

"What? Do I think the police suspect me?"

"That's what I was going to ask, yes."

"Probably," he said. "She had my name on her, and she was found behind the hotel . . ."

"But that's not enough evidence?"

"No, but there's one more thing."

"What's that?"

"They don't have any other suspects."

"Well, maybe Roper can find the younger sister," Melanie offered.

"Maybe," Clint said, "but she already thinks I killed her father. Now she's going to think I killed her sister, too."

"And that bothers you?"

"Yes, it does."

Suddenly, she seemed embarrassed.

"I'm sorry I asked that question. It's just . . ."

"You know my reputation."

"Yes," she said, "but now, having spent just this little time with you, I can't imagine that half of the things I heard are true."

"Well, that's probably about right," he said. "Half of it is probably true, but no one knows any of the circumstances. All anyone ever hears is the outcome."

"It's unfair," she said. "I know I've heard things about Roper that aren't true, as well."

The waiter came and collected their plates and took their dessert orders.

"So what will you do now?" she asked.

"Work with Roper, try to find the girl," Clint said. "Convince her that I didn't kill her father or her sister, and try to convince her not to kill me."

"Well," she said, "I know I only shuffle papers in Roper's office, but if there's anything I can do . . ."

"I appreciate the offer, Melanie," he said. "I might take you up on it."

He tried to change the subject over dessert, but he soon realized there was little else on either of their minds.

After they finished their desserts, Clint paid the bill and walked with Melanie back to the hotel, where he figured to put her into a cab.

Dirk Wilson slapped the naked ass in front of him, then slid his rigid penis up between the girl's thighs and into her pussy. The girl grunted because Wilson's thrust was violent.

"God," she said, groaning as he started to pound into her.

"Complainin', bitch?" he asked, slapping her ass again.

"No, no," she said, "give it to me hard, Dirk . . . harder."

"I'll give it to you hard, bitch," Wilson said, grunting with the effort.

"Come on, come on . . ." she moaned, slamming her butt back into him to meet each of his thrusts.

He reached out one hand to grab hold of her long black hair. The other hand he rubbed over her sweaty butt cheeks. He yanked on her hair as he continued to fuck her, stretching her neck, but still no complaint from her.

"Come on," she cried out, "you can do better than that!"

"You bet I can, you dirty slut."

He took his penis out of her, glistening with her juices, then spread her ass cheeks and drove himself into her ass. He'd never done this with any woman before, but she had shown him, and she loved it.

"How's this, bitch?" he asked, slamming into her. "Huh? How do you like this?"

"Is that all you got?" she squeezed out, clenching her teeth.

He knew he was ripping her ass, he knew it hurt, but the bitch would never admit it. He'd never known a woman who liked it so hard.

"Come on," she cried out, "make it hurt, damnit! Hurt me!"

He continued to fuck her ass, slapping her buttocks until they glowed hot and red. Finally, he erupted inside her, let his weight fall on top of her as he fought to catch his breath.

"That was better," she said from beneath him. "Now get the hell off me!"

THIRTEEN

"Are you still foolin' with that girl?"

Wilson looked over his shoulder at the dark-haired girl in the bed with him. He'd never known a girl who liked sex so much or so hard, and his dick was sore from keeping her satisfied.

"It's my job," he said. "You know that."

Rita laughed.

"She ain't never gonna let you fuck 'er, Dirk," she said nastily. "Not that little Miss Priss."

"You're crazy, you know that?" he said. "I don't wanna fuck her."

"Sure you do," Rita said. She pulled her knees up to her breasts, starting to pick at something on her toe. "She's just the type all men wanna fuck, but won't get to. You ain't no different."

"Aw hell . . ." he said, getting up and grabbing his clothes.

"And she sure as hell ain't gonna let you fuck her in the ass," Rita added.

"Nobody does that but you, Rita," he said. "That's 'cause you're dirty."

"You bet I am," Rita said, "but don't kid yerself. I ain't the only one. There's plenty of girls like me. You just ain't met them. You know why?"

Wilson didn't answer.

"It's because you ain't dirty enough," she said. "A real man's gotta get dirty to have good sex. And rough."

"I give it to you rough."

"You gotta get rougher," Rita said, getting to her knees. Her big, pear-shaped tits swayed as she moved. "And you gotta come up with some other words. Ya can't just keep callin' me a bitch."

"You are a bitch."

Rita laughed.

"Of course I am," she said. "If you treated yer gal like a dirty bitch, maybe you'd get somewhere with her."

"She's not my gal," Wilson said. "You are."

"Don't kid yerself, Dirk," she said. "You ain't the only cowboy stickin' your dick up my ass."

"Rita, damnit!"

"Did that hurt yer feelin's, honey?"

She put her arms around his chest from behind as he sat on the bed pulling on his boots.

"You want to be Mama's only man?"

He shrugged her off.

"You can fuck anybody you want," he said, standing up. "It don't matter to me."

She pouted, pushing out her full lower lip. She was a tall, big-breasted girl with skinny arms and legs and a lot of black hair. Her breasts had large, dark brown nipples that fascinated him. She wasn't young, probably his age, just over thirty. She was so different from Laura Kellogg, and he suspected that was why Laura interested him, because of the difference. Laura was young and innocent, even though she was on a mission to kill Clint Adams. He still thought if he helped her he might win her over, but he was sure she had never had sex in her life. She would never do the things Rita did.

Funny, it was Laura's innocence that drew him to her, while it was Rita's willingness to do anything in bed that drew him to her.

"I'll see you later, Rita," he said, heading for the door.

"Where you goin'?"

"I've gotta see my boss."

"And then back to Miss Priss?"

"I guess," he said. "Whatever the boss says."

"Well, don't forget," she said, lying back on the bed and spreading her legs for him, "I'll be here."

Wilson knew he was going to have to come up with some new words to describe just how dirty Rita was.

Wilson left the building Rita lived in. It was near the docks where the rents were cheap. The one thing Rita never did was ask him for money for her rent. Was she getting it from someone else? he wondered.

And what did that matter? She was just a whore. Sure, she didn't charge him for what they did, but she was a whore, anyway. Who else would let him— make him—do the things he did to her?

But Laura Kellogg, now she was a young girl who could very easily become a lady. All he had to do was play the situation right, keep everyone happy, and maybe he'd have a chance with her.

Today he had to tell her that her sister was dead, probably killed by Clint Adams. That was after he went to see his boss.

The one thing he had to make sure Laura never found out was that he was the one who had actually killed her sister and left her behind the Denver House to implicate Clint Adams.

FOURTEEN

Clint woke the next morning alone. He'd been sorely tempted to invite Melanie back to his room, but thought better of it. He wasn't sure she'd accept, and she might have thought badly of him for the invitation after only one meal together.

He got out of bed slowly, as he thought sadly about poor Rose Kellogg lying behind the hotel in the garbage. He decided to have a quick breakfast and then find Roper and discuss the situation with him. He decided Rose's death had to have something to do with her sister's desire to kill him.

Coincidence was his least favorite word in the English language, and he wouldn't believe that until it was proven to him. He washed using the pitcher and basin on the dresser, dressed, strapped on his gun, and went downstairs.

He took his breakfast in the Denver House dining room, which was excellent, then went out front and got a cab to Roper's office.

When he entered the office, Melanie looked up at him and smiled.

"Under the circumstances is it all right if I say I enjoyed last night?" she asked, keeping her voice low.

"It's very all right," he said.

"I haven't said anything to Roper about Rose Kellogg," she said. "He would have wanted to know how I heard about it."

"That's good, thanks," he said. "Is he alone?"

"Yes," she said. "I'm sure you can go right in."

"Thanks."

He knocked, then opened the door and entered. Roper looked up at him in surprise.

"So," he said, "she's already letting you in without checking first. It didn't take you long."

"She's a nice lady," Clint said, "and she knows we're friends."

"I've got news," Roper said.

"About Laura Kellogg?"

Roper shook his head.

"The sister, Rose," he said. "I'm afraid she's dead—unless, of course, you already know that."

"I do," Clint said. "When did you find out?"

"This morning," Roper said. "I have a contact. How did you find out?"

"The police came and got me."

Clint told Roper about Rose Kellogg having his name on her.

"Was it her handwriting?"

"I don't know," Clint said. "I didn't see it, and I wouldn't have been able to tell, anyway. Why?"

"Somebody's tryin' to frame you."

"So you don't think it's a coincidence?"

"No," Roper said, "and neither do you. I know how you feel about that word."

"This can't be the girl," Clint said.

"I don't think so, either," Roper said. "This is a plan. It probably started with the girl, but somebody's using her."

"I agree," Clint said.

"So . . . who?"

"The list is long," Clint said.

"Well, I know a lot of people want to kill you, Clint," Roper said, "but how many of them won't do it themselves?"

"That would cut the list down a bit," Clint said. "There's quite a few of them who would like to do it themselves."

"So, while I continue to try to locate the Kellogg girl, you'll have to try to come up with a list of people who want you dead," Roper explained, "who would likely be in this part of the country, and who would most likely hire it done."

"That's not going to be easy," Clint said. "And why this part of the country? They could be from anywhere. Maybe they came here, or maybe they're dealing with someone by telegraph."

"Well, we've got to shorten the list somehow," Roper said. "You'll also need to come up with someone who would not only want to kill you, but make you suffer. Like framing you for Rose Kellogg's murder."

"Okay," Clint said, "but I'd also like to do something more active."

"Good," Roper said, "because I've got somethin' more active for you to do."

"And what's that?"

"Try stayin' alive."

FIFTEEN

Dirk Wilson entered the office and looked at his boss, seated behind his cherrywood desk.

"About time," the man said. "I've got work to do, you know."

"Sorry, sir."

"What've you got for me?"

"The Kellogg woman is dead."

"Good. And the Gunsmith?"

"I left his name on her body, written on a slip of paper."

"Your handwriting?"

Wilson shook his head.

"Her sister's," he said, "but it looks like hers."

"How did you get the sister to write it?"

"It wasn't hard," Wilson said with a smirk. "She pretty much does whatever I tell her."

"That's good," his boss said. "Keep it that way."

"Yes, sir," Wilson said, "but when do we let her loose on him?"

"We don't," the other man said. "I didn't set this all up just to let some fool girl kill him."

"She's not gonna like that."

"I don't give a good goddamn what she likes, and neither should you," the man said. "As long as I'm paying you, you care what *I* say."

"Yes, sir."

"I'm going to have a talk with the detective who's going to be working on the girl's murder. Meanwhile, you tell your girlfriend that her sister is dead, probably killed by the Gunsmith."

"I don't mean to question you, sir," Wilson said, "but why are we getting her all riled up if we ain't gonna let her kill him?"

"Never mind," the other man said. "You just work on keeping her happy. I'm sure you know how to do that, right?"

"Oh, yes, sir," Wilson said with a wink. "I'm keepin' her real happy, and tired out."

"I'm sure you are. You can go now. I'll be in touch soon."

"Yes, sir. Uh, sir?"

"Yes?"

"I need some, uh, I mean, I could use some—"

"Oh, all right." The man opened a desk drawer, took out some money, and handed it across the desk. "Make that last."

"Yes, sir." Wilson put it in his pocket without counting it, turned, and headed for the door.

"On your way out, send in my secretary."

"Yes, sir."

* * *

The woman came in, stood in front of the desk, and
didn't say a word. She was in her midfifties and had
been working for her boss for fifteen years. She knew
when to speak and when not to.

"Is Carver in town, Helen?"

"I believe so, sir."

"Find out for sure."

"Yes, sir."

"And get him here as soon as possible."

"Yes, sir."

"And get word to my wife that I'll be home late tonight."

She kept her face impassive as she said, "Yes, sir."
She knew if he was going home late it meant he was
going to see his mistress. She didn't approve, but she
couldn't very well say anything, since she had been
his mistress for five years when she first started working for him.

"That's all, Helen."

"Yes, sir."

She turned, left the room, and returned to her desk.

Rita got herself ready for her banker boyfriend. She'd
only been half lying to Dirk Wilson when she told
him he wasn't the only one sticking his dick up her
ass. He was the only one—except for the banker.

She kept Wilson on a string because the banker
was older, and could only perform half the time. The
younger man never failed to provide a nice, stiff dick
for her amusement.

The banker was the one who supplied her with money, which, sometimes, was more important than a stiff body part.

Rita stood at her window and looked down at the street. She didn't know what Wilson was trying to pull with his young Miss Priss, but she knew something was up. She'd find out eventually, and maybe there'd be a way for her to make some money from it. What she'd really like to do was leave Denver, leave both Wilson and the banker behind, and go make a life for herself someplace like San Francisco.

But that was for later. Later that day, it would be banker time.

SIXTEEN

Keeping himself alive was always uppermost in the mind of the Gunsmith. He didn't have to be told that, but he knew Roper was concerned about him.

"What you should probably do," his friend said, "is lock yourself in your room and stay away from all the windows."

"Yeah," Clint said, "I could do that for the rest of my life. And so could you. You've probably got almost as many people ready to kill you as I do."

Roper grinned and said, "Maybe, but not as many women."

"Ha ha. I'm not staying in my room, Tal."

"I didn't think so," Roper said, "but it was worth the suggestion."

"What about the police?" Clint asked. "Do you know who is working on this?"

"Nobody you know," Roper said. "It's a detective named Shane, Mike Shane."

"I talked to a sergeant named O'Malley."

"Yeah, he's been around for a while," Roper said. "Not too smart, not too honest . . ."

"But?"

"No buts," Roper said. "That's it."

"Great," Clint said. "What about this Shane? Is he just going to go after me because I'm standing in front of him?"

"Probably," Roper said. "He's a good detective, but like O'Malley, he's not particularly honest. If his boss tells him to key on you, he's not about to use his imagination."

Clint realized that was one thing that made his friend a great detective—he had imagination. He looked beyond the obvious.

"I'm going to pass the word around town that I need some information," Roper said. "My contacts should be getting back to me soon."

"And what if they get back to you with . . . nothing?" Clint asked.

"We'll have to deal with that when the time comes," Roper said. "Let's not go lookin' for trouble before we have to."

"I never have to go looking for trouble, Tal," Clint said, standing up. "You know that."

Roper did know that. On the one hand he felt that Clint had brought that on himself because of his reputation. On the other hand he felt it was through no fault of his friend that he had this reputation. It was a double-edged sword. There had to have been a time during Clint Adams's life when a different decision, a changed direction, might have changed things for good.

Roper got up and walked with Clint to his office door.

"I know you won't stay in your room," he said, "but maybe you should change hotels."

"Believe me, that won't help," Clint said. "If somebody wants to find me, they will. I might as well be in a place like the Denver House, where anybody can't just walk in off the street.

"Okay," Tal said with a sigh. "I'll do my best to help you on this, Clint."

"I know you will, Tal," Clint said. "I sure appreciate it."

"Don't thank me until we see if I have any success," he said.

"You'll send me a bill?"

"Yeah," Roper answered with a look that said, don't be stupid. "Get out."

Roper pushed him out and closed the door behind him.

Laura Kellogg listened to the news from Dirk Wilson, feeling her insides grow colder and colder.

"My God," she said when he was finished, "the man's a monster."

"Laura—"

"I have to kill him," she said. "I have to. Not just for me and my family, but for the country."

It was a mark of how young she was that she was being so dramatic.

"And you will," he said, "but in a way that you won't have to pay for it. I mean, he should be killed, but you don't want to go to jail for it."

"Why not?" she asked. "What's the difference? I have no family left."

"There must be somebody back East," Wilson said. "Look, this is a shock. Don't make any decisions until we think it over and talk about it."

"Sure, Dirk," she said, staring dully ahead of her. "Sure. We'll think about it."

SEVENTEEN

When Woodrow Carver walked into the banker's office, the man behind the desk was surprised, but he shouldn't have been. Helen was usually very efficient, and she had managed to get Carver there within two hours of his request.

"Carver."

The gunman sat down opposite the banker without a word.

"Things are going according to plan," the banker told Carver.

"This is about the Gunsmith?"

"What else have we been planning?" the banker asked.

Carver fell silent.

"I want to make sure you're staying in town," the banker said. "I'm going to need you on this."

"You're payin' the freight," Carver told him. "I'll be around."

"Okay," the banker said, "but be where Helen can find you fast."

"She's pretty good at findin' me," Carver said.

"Just stay available and stay out of trouble."

"As long as you're payin' me," Carver reminded the man again, "I ain't plannin' on no trouble."

"You may not be planning on it, but men like you attract it," the banker said. "Just . . . don't, is what I'm saying."

"Maybe you oughta toss a little more cash my way, just to make sure."

The banker had anticipated this request. He opened his drawer, took out an envelope, and passed it over, the same thing he had done with Dirk Wilson earlier.

Unlike Wilson, Carver counted the money, then left it in the envelope and tucked it away in a pocket.

"That keep you out of trouble?" the banker asked.

"Just might," Carver said.

"That's all," the banker said. "Just stay where I can get to you."

"That all?" Carver asked.

"That's it."

Carver unwound rather than stood from the chair, the way tall men did. He started for the door, then stopped and turned.

"What hotel is Adams stayin' in?"

"Why?" the banker asked.

"No reason."

The banker hesitated, then said, "I'm going to tell you, because I know it wouldn't be hard for you to find out." He gestured with his pencil. "But don't go after him until I say so, or you'll be doing it for free. Understand?"

"I understand."

"He's at the Denver House."

"Nice place."

"Yes, it is," the banker said. "The kind of place the likes of you can't just go walking into. Remember that."

"You're the boss," Carver said.

"Yes, well," the banker said, "remember that, too."

Carver opened the door and stepped out.

As Carver exited her boss's office, Helen looked up at him. She knew he was about forty, roughly ten years her junior, but she still felt a tingle whenever she saw him.

"Woodrow," she said.

"Helen."

Carver came to the desk, placed his roughhewn hand over her smooth one.

"See you tonight?" he asked.

"Oh, yes," she said breathlessly.

He smiled at her and left the office. His scent stayed behind, a hard, masculine scent that she enjoyed having on her sheets after he left her bed.

She felt a flush creep up into her face. At fifty she was having the best sex of her life with a man she never would have looked at twenty years ago. But then, twenty years ago she wasn't the experienced woman she was now. At that point she hadn't been the banker's mistress yet, and for thirty was remarkably unschooled as far as sex was concerned. Perhaps not unschooled for that time, but certainly for this.

Helen Kramer had never felt as alive as she did now, at fifty.

As Carver left the bank building, he was thinking not about the banker, or about Clint Adams, but about Helen. For a man who had spent most of his life getting sex from whores, she was an amazing find for him. She was exactly the kind of woman who would never have looked at him on the street, and who he would never have looked at. If someone had told him he would one day be sharing the bed of a fifty-year-old woman, he would have told them they were crazy— unless, of course, he was sixty at the time.

But at forty he had tired of whores, and he found younger women silly and stupid.

And, of course, there was the added factor of her working for the banker. He knew much more of the man's business than he should have. In fact, he knew almost everything she did, which was—in some cases—probably even more than the banker himself knew.

At some point, Carver, who knew that the banker thought of him as a mindless gunman, would turn that knowledge to good use.

He enjoyed knowing that he was taking the man's money, bedding his secretary, and apparently following his orders to the letter while making life-changing plans of his own.

A man could not live by his gun forever, and at forty Woodrow Carver was finally turning his brain into a useful weapon, one that complemented his gun nicely.

There had been a time when he would have charged right over to the Gunsmith's hotel, challenged him, and probably been killed for his trouble. However, now he decided to go over to the Denver House and see if he couldn't have a look at the famous Gunsmith, just for the purpose of more information.

EIGHTEEN

Sid Black was a gambler. Clint had met him when he had a gambling hall on Harrison Street in Leadville. Now he was plying his trade in Denver, with a hall near the Palace Theater.

The thing Clint knew about Sid Black was that, no matter where Sid lived, he ended up with contacts. When Clint left Talbot Roper's office, he went straight to Sid Black's Arcade Theater, which offered everything from whiskey to gambling to dancing girls.

The front door was locked, as it was too early for the place to be open. Clint pounded on the door until a wild-eyed man with a massive mane of black hair and a beard opened it.

"We're closed, damnit!" the man shouted.

"Even to old friends?"

The man narrowed his eyes. Suddenly, his eyes brightened and white teeth showed from behind the beard.

"Clint Adams, by God!"

The man stepped out and grabbed Clint in a bear

hug, lifting him off the floor. Sid Black was about six five and wide rather than fat.

"You're going to kill me!" Clint managed to gurgle. "Put me down."

"Come on in, you old scudder," Black said, pulling Clint inside and closing the door again.

"Come to the bar! This calls for a drink."

Black led Clint through the massive room to the bar. In the front of the room was a large stage, and across the floor were covered gaming tables.

"What'll ya have? Beer?" Black asked, getting behind the bar.

"It's kind of early—"

"It's cold, and free."

"Beer sounds good."

Black drew two beers, slid one over to Clint, and the two men drank.

"Jesus, the last time I saw you," Black said with beer foam dripping from his beard, "you were tryin' not to kill Jules Handler in Leadville."

"He deserved killing," Clint said. "But you're right, I resisted."

"Well, he only lasted another week after you left," Black said. "Some drifter gunned him."

"It was only a matter of time."

"Ah, it's good to see you, Clint. Whataya doin' in Denver?"

"I just sort of drifted this way, Sid, but it looks like I drifted into some trouble."

"You? Trouble? What're the chances?" Black laughed a big booming laugh, then looked embarrassed. "Sorry. What can I do to help?"

Clint had gone over a few scenarios in his head, a way to explain the situation to Sid Black without it getting too complicated.

"Somebody in Denver is trying to frame me for murder." This was the part of the story he'd decided to tell.

"Who are you supposed to've murdered?"

"A woman named Rose Kellogg," Clint said. "Her body was found behind the Denver House hotel."

"And that's where you're stayin'?"

"Yes."

"Did you know her?"

"Yes, but not well. We'd only met the day before."

"Was she one of your . . ." Black wiggled his big bushy eyebrows.

"No, Sid. I told you we only just met."

"That never stopped you in Leadville."

"This is not the same."

"Okay, then," Sid said. "What can I do? How can I help you find the bastard?"

"It's got to be someone who hates me, but doesn't just want to come right out and kill me. He—or she—wants me to suffer."

"I guess what they'd really like, then, is for you to get arrested for this murder. What're you doin' to keep that from happenin'?"

"I've got Talbot Roper working on that."

"Wow, you don't fool around," Black said. "He's a big gun, costs a lot of money."

"We're friends," Clint said. "He's trying to help."

"Well, I'll do the same then," Black offered. "Least I can do. You saved my ass a few times in Leadville."

Clint hadn't brought that up himself, but he'd been hoping the man would remember.

"Okay, Sid."

"Come back tonight, watch the girls," Black said. "I'll see what I can find out."

"Okay."

Black walked him to the door.

"Don't figure on eatin' here, though," he added. "Food's lousy. I haven't found myself a good cook yet."

"I'll make sure I eat first."

Outside, Black slapped Clint on the back hard enough to take his breath away.

"Great to see ya, Clint," Black said. "We'll find this bastard for ya!"

NINETEEN

Clint now had both Talbot Roper and the gambler Sid Black working for his benefit. But Denver was a big place—a city, not a town—and while the odds of finding men or women who hated him were not short, finding the specific man or woman who was plotting against him did offer short odds.

It was only recently that a plot had been hatched against Clint while he was in New Orleans. Now he had run into what appeared to be another one. He much preferred the direct approach, when somebody came up to him face-to-face and challenged him. He hated bushwhackers and backshooters, but where did this rate? He had Rose Kellogg's word that her sister, Laura, had been the one taking shots at him over the past month, but now it seemed much more thought had gone into this than simply bushwhacking him. There was somebody behind this with imagination, and while Clint normally appreciated people like that, he didn't like being this confused about what was going on. He preferred to have the imaginative people working for him, not against him.

Roper had imagination *and* intelligence, and this was his town. So maybe the detective would be able to figure this all out. His advice to Clint to lock himself in his room was good advice, it just wasn't something Clint felt he could do.

So if he was going to be out and about, what could he be doing, other than making a target of himself?

What about the younger sister? What was she going to do when she heard about her sister's death? What was her part in this grand plan? And why was she part of it? And would she keep playing her part now that her sister was dead, or come after him?

There was a man standing at the front desk as Clint entered the hotel lobby, and the clerk spoke quickly and pointed to him. The other man nodded and came walking up to intercept Clint.

He was a tall man, midthirties, wearing the kind of tailored suit Clint never had a taste for.

"Clint Adams?"

"That's right."

"My name is Shane," the man said. "Detective." He showed Clint his badge. "I have some questions for you about Rose Kellogg. The woman who was killed—"

"I know who she is."

"Was," Shane corrected him. "Where can we do this? Your room?"

"Why don't we get a drink?"

"Suits me," Shane said. "Let's go."

Clint led the way to the hotel bar.

"Beer?" Clint asked.

"Good enough."

Clint went to the bar while the detective chose a table. There were plenty to pick from, as the place was almost empty. Clint carried two beers back to the table and put one in front of the detective.

"Thanks," Shane said. "What do I owe you?"

"Forget it."

Clint sat across from the man and waited.

"I talked with Talbot Roper this morning," Shane said. "Or, rather, he talked to me. Told me you and him were good friends."

"We are."

"He also wanted me to know you don't go around killing women."

"I don't."

"And that even if you did, you wouldn't strangle them."

Clint didn't know what to say to that.

"Guess he figures you'd just shoot 'em, huh?"

Clint remained silent.

"In any case, I need to hear from you how you came to meet Miss Kellogg."

Clint told him about meeting Rose Kellogg, and he decided to go ahead and tell the detective about Laura Kellogg, because the fact that Laura had been taking shots at him was a possible motive for him to kill Laura, not Rose.

"So Miss Kellogg wanted to warn you about her sister?" Shane asked.

"Yes," Clint said, "but she also asked for my help to stop her sister, and get her back home."

"So this other Miss Kellogg, Laura," Shane said, "is still out there."

"Right."

"So she's probably gonna keep tryin' to kill you, especially after she hears about her sister's death."

"That's what I think."

"So what are you plannin' to do?"

"Find her, if I can," Clint said, "and convince her I didn't kill her sister."

"And what about her father?"

"I didn't kill him, either."

"Why does she think you did?"

"It apparently has something to do with her mother," Clint said. "She told her daughters all their lives that I killed her husband."

"Why did she do that?"

"I don't know," Clint said, "and we can't ask her because she passed away about four years ago."

"So the father died twenty years ago, the mother four, and now the sister," Shane said. "Has this girl got any family left?"

"I don't know that," Clint said. "I assume there's somebody back East."

Shane took a quick sip from the beer, left the rest, and stood up.

"Well, it seems to me you didn't have much motive to kill Rose Kellogg."

"I'm glad to hear you say that."

"Of course, that's assuming you're tellin' me the whole truth."

"Of course."

"I guess you should hope the younger sister doesn't show up dead," Shane said, "because you've got a hell of a motive to want her dead, don't you?"

The detective left before Clint could say a word.

TWENTY

Before Clint could get up and leave the bar, Talbot Roper came walking in.

"I saw Shane leavin'," he said, joining Clint, "figured you were in here. Whose is this?" Roper indicated the almost untouched beer in front of him.

Clint almost said it was Shane's, but instead he said, "That's yours." He figured, what was the harm? The police detective had hardly touched it.

Clint reached across the table and rotated the mug, moving the handle from Roper's left to his right.

"You were expecting me?" Roper asked.

"I have some contacts, too," Clint lied. "A bellboy saw you come in."

"Good," Roper said, reaching for the beer, "because I need this." He grabbed the beer and drank down half of it. "Ahhhh . . ."

"Sounds like you've been working hard," Clint said.

"Day and night," Roper said.

"And what do you have to show for it?"

"Not much."

"Then why are you here?"

"I wanted to tell you that I had a talk with Shane," Roper said, "but I guess he beat me to it."

"He did."

"Well . . . we could get some lunch. You wanna have some lunch?"

"Where?"

"Right here," Roper said. "We're here and I'm hungry now. They have a great dining room, right?"

"Yes."

"Well, come on," Roper said. "I can at least tell you what I've been doin', and then you can tell me."

"What makes you think I've been doing anything?" Clint asked. "For all you know I've been sitting in my room like you suggested."

"That'll be the day," Roper said. "I know you, Clint. I'll bet you reached out to some gambling buddy of yours for some help."

Clint didn't answer.

"Am I right?"

"Shut up," Clint said, getting up. "Let's go and get some lunch."

TWENTY-ONE

Over lunch Roper told Clint about the contacts he'd called upon for information. They were men and women who lived and worked in Denver, from the docks to the business district.

"I'm still waiting to hear from some," he said, "but the ones I've heard from so far have no information that has anything to do with you. They all recognized your name, but they don't know anything beyond that."

"I talked to Sid Black," Clint said. "He said he'd put out some feelers and see what he could come up with."

"Black, the gambler?" Roper said. "I should've known. Where did you meet him?"

"Leadville," Clint said. "He had a place on Harrison Street for a while. Now he's here, down near the Palace Theater."

"What's his place called?"

"The Arcade Theater."

"I know it," Roper said. "Yeah, he could have some contacts I don't have. Between us, though, we probably have the town covered. Let me know if he comes up with anything."

"Maybe you guys should get together, compare notes," Clint said. "I'm going over there tonight to check out his operation. You want to come along?"

"Sure, why not?" Roper replied. "I could do with seeing some dancing girls."

"Couldn't we all."

They left the dining room and stopped in the lobby.

"I'll come by with a cab tonight," Roper said. "Nine okay?"

"Fine. Eat something first, though. Black says his cook is terrible."

"I'll grab something earlier," Roper said. "Maybe you could have another supper with my secretary."

"She told you?"

"No," Roper said, "you just did, but I knew it. I know you, Clint. I know you real well. And I know Melanie, even though she's only worked for me for a short time. I knew she was hiding something from me."

"All we did was eat."

"If you say so," Roper said. "I'll see you at nine."

Roper left the hotel, and Clint, for want of something else to do, went to his room. There was really nothing for him to do until he and Roper went to see Sid Black.

When they got to Sid Black's Arcade Theater, the place was ablaze with light and alive with music and noise. Voices were raised in singing, laughing, and shouting.

"How can anyone gamble in this racket?" Roper asked.

"I'm sure he's got some private rooms for the serious gamblers," Clint said.

They entered the Arcade and their senses were assailed at every turn. But just as they got their bearings, the girls on stage completed a number, the music stopped, and the curtain closed. Now the only sounds were those of a normal saloon—voices, glasses clinking, chips falling.

"That's better," Roper said as they approached the bar.

"What can I get you gents?" the bartender asked. Clint remembered him from Leadville, but not his name.

"Two beers, and Sid," Clint said. "My name's Clint Adams."

"Yeah, yeah," the man said. "Sid told me you was comin'. We met in Leadville, Mr. Adams. My name's Boris."

Boris was in his late fifties, as bald as Sid Black was hairy.

"I remember, Boris," Clint said.

"I'll tell Sid you're here," Boris said. He put two beers in front of them and said, "On the house. You just missed the girls, but they'll be on again soon."

They picked up their beers and turned their backs to the bar. There were no expensive furnishings in the place, but it was still impressive in its size and scope. It was a much larger operation than Sid had had in Leadville.

"Clint!" Sid Black's voice boomed. Both he and

Roper turned and saw the big man bearing down on them. "And you'd be Talbot Roper, right?"

"Right."

Instead of hugging Clint as he had done earlier, he settled for crushing both their hands with his.

"I hope Boris gave you those beers on the house," the big man said.

"He did."

"Then I won't fire his ass," Black said, and laughed. "You just missed the girls, but they'll be on again in ten minutes."

"I may have to be gone by then," Roper said. "I just wanted to see if you had time to compare some notes."

"Notes?"

"Clint says you're going to try to help him," Roper said. "We might compare contacts."

"I don't think you know any of my contacts," Black said. "They'd be a little low-class for you."

"I go as low as I have to, Mr. Black."

"Just call me Sid."

"Also, I'm not as high-class as you think I am."

"We better go to my office and talk there," Black said. "It'll be quieter when the music starts up again. Follow me."

"Clint?" Roper said.

"I'm going to stay here," he said. "You let me know what happens."

"Bring your beer, Mr. Roper," Black said, and led the way to the back of the huge room.

True to Sid Black's word the girls came on again while he and Roper were still in his office. Clint ordered a second beer and moved to the front of the room so he could see better. Men were stomping their feet and clapping their hands as the girls raised their skirts and showed their legs while they danced. Roper was right, this was not the place he'd ever come to for gambling. Even in a private room, he bet they could hear this music.

But to see pretty girls flashing their legs, this was the ideal place.

TWENTY-TWO

Roper and Black returned after the girls went off stage again. Clint had finished his second beer, but had not ordered another one.

"You fellas done?"

"Turns out we do know some of the same people," Roper said as they left. Sid Black had mashed both their hands again and said he'd be in touch as soon as he found out anything.

"If somebody in Denver wants you dead, I'll hear about it," he promised.

Outside, he and Roper caught another cab and pulled away from the Arcade. Roper explained who some of the people were that he and Black had in common.

"Turns out I'm really not as high-class as he thinks I am," the detective finished.

They dropped Roper off first. As he climbed down from the cab, he said, "Keep your eyes open. And I mean, watch out for Shane as much as anyone else."

"He said he didn't think I had a motive for killing Rose."

"Right," Roper replied. "Just watch out, all right?"

"Okay, Tal."

As Clint entered his hotel room, his senses told him someone was there. He could smell perfume in the air, hear the rustle of the sheets on his bed. He could feel the presence of another person, but his instincts told him there was no danger.

He turned the light up on the gas lamp on the wall and saw the woman lying in his bed.

"I convinced a bellboy to let me in," Melanie said. "I hope you don't mind."

"No," Clint said. "I don't mind."

"I'm also naked under this sheet," she said. "I hope you don't mind that, either."

"I don't mind that at all."

"Well then . . ."

She tossed the sheet back to show him just how naked she was.

She had long lovely legs, a tangle of auburn hair between them, and high, small breasts that were well rounded and tipped with dark brown nipples.

"Hurry," she said. "I've been waiting awhile and I'm impatient."

"I have to say I'm a little . . . surprised by this," he said, unbuttoning his shirt.

"Oh? Why?" she asked. "Couldn't you tell I was attracted to you?"

"Well . . . I hoped so, but you're such a . . ."

"A what?"

"A lady."

She laughed, a throaty, sexy sound.

"And ladies don't have sex?"

"I just didn't think . . . didn't know if . . . well, this soon . . ."

"For a man experienced with women you're stammering quite a bit."

"I'm sorry—"

"Don't be," she said. "I think it's very cute."

"Cute . . ."

"Now come on," she said. "Hurry up and get those clothes off, get in this bed, and make love to me. And don't forget . . ."

"Don't forget what?"

"To take off that gun," she said. "I don't want to get shot by accident."

Carver watched Helen undress for him. For a woman her age she had a fine body. She had heavy breasts, wide hips, and smooth, pale skin. She was past her prime, he knew, but to him she was beautiful.

Not that he was any great catch. He knew he had big ears and a long jaw. No woman had ever called him handsome, or even good-looking. But Helen, she told him all sorts of things about himself. Not that he believed them, but they were nice to hear.

Naked, she came to him as he sat on the bed. She took his head and cradled it between her warm breasts. He kissed her warm flesh, licked her nipples while she ran her fingers through his hair.

He was naked and his erection sprang up between them. She sank down to her knees, took him in her hands, and rubbed the smooth, heavily veined column of flesh over her cheeks. He ran his hands over her shoulders and back while she began to kiss and lick his penis, crooning to it, fondling it, and finally engulfing him in her hot, wet mouth.

The banker was more than up to the task today.

He'd no sooner arrived than he'd whipped off his pants to show her a raging erection. She thought he looked not only harder, but larger than she'd ever seen him.

He was also more aggressive, practically tearing off her clothes and throwing her down on the bed. He straddled her and drove himself into her while she was still dry, so it was more than a little painful. She didn't really mind, though. She became wet very quickly and they were soon grunting and groaning with the effort of their fucking. She knew he'd never been this way with his wife. Not with that dried-up old prune.

Then he surprised her by saying, "Turn over."

"I thought you didn't like that—" she started, but he roughly turned her over and spread her ass cheeks. Normally she had to talk him into this, but here he was bulling his way into her from behind.

"Wait, wait," she said, "you're hurting me . . ."

"You like it when it hurts," he growled. "You tell me that all the time."

"Yes, but—"

He pushed her head down into her pillow, entered her roughly, and began pounding away.

TWENTY-THREE

Melanie was no lady in bed.

As soon as Clint was naked and had joined her, she dove between his legs, took hold of his erection, and began to make love to it. She used her hands, her mouth, her tongue, her teeth. She brought him to the brink of orgasm several times, until he was painfully swollen.

He reached down for her and pulled her up.

"Time for me to return the favor," he said.

He got down between her legs and lovingly ministered to her for fifteen minutes or so. She trembled and cried out several times, her heels pounding uncontrollably on the bed. He licked her and sucked her until she cried out, and then cried, and finally waves of pleasure rolled over her, causing her to push him away and roll over on her side.

"Wait, wait," she gasped, holding one hand out to him, "you're killing me."

"Like I said," Clint responded, "I was just returning the favor."

*   *   *

Helen sat astride her lover, the outlaw gunman. She rode him hard, sweat running down her body, her breath coming in raspy gulps. He moved his hips in unison with hers, coming up to meet her every time she came down on him.

She stared down at him, gazed at his face, enjoyed the way his eyes closed, the way he bit his lip, the power she had at that moment over this man she knew killed with his gun for money.

It was exciting, as it always was. Her lovers—what few there had been in her life—had always been gentlemen, or businessmen like her boss. She had never been married, never even been proposed to. Her sex life had been moribund at best for years, until the day this man, Woodrow Carver, walked into the office.

The day their eyes met, her whole life changed, and she knew the same was true for him.

She felt her legs and thighs begin to tremble, leaned down so that her breasts were in his face. He kissed them, bit her nipples. They had not been having sex for a very long period of time, but they'd had sex many times, and he knew when she was ready, and he knew she liked for him to be on top when her time came.

Roughly, he flipped her onto her back.

"Get out!" Rita said.

"Rita, wait—"

He reached out to her, but she pulled away from him, curled up against the wall.

"You're crazy," she said.

"But you said you liked it hard—"

"I said hard," she said. "I didn't say anythin' about rippin' me up!" She looked down at the blood on the sheet. There wasn't a lot of it, but enough to make her good and angry.

"Rita, I'm sorry," he said. "I was just . . . so excited—"

"Foreclose on somebody today, banker?" she asked. "Go on, get out, and don't come back. Go home to your wife and see if she'll let you fuck her from now on."

"Rita—"

"Get out!" she screamed at him.

Sheepishly, all his passion spent, the banker dressed and slunk out the door.

Rita decided she needed a bath . . . and maybe a doctor.

Clint watched as Melanie went down between his legs again, took him in her mouth, and sucked him wetly until he was as swollen as he'd ever been. Then she mounted him, rubbed her juices over the length of him, reached down, took hold of him, and guided him into her.

She was hot, wet, and very slick as she began to ride him up and down. Her breath came in sibilant hisses as she drove herself down on him, grinding for a moment, and then rising back up only to come down again.

Clint held her by the hips, the waist, then slid his hands up to cup her breasts. Her head was back, her eyes closed, giving him a fine view of the lovely lines of her neck.

He used his thumbs on her nipples and she bit her lip and moaned. She had her hands pressed down on him, using him for balance and purchase. As he felt his own release building he began to move his hips with her, so that the room filled with the sound of their damp flesh slapping together.

"Oh, God, yes . . ." she moaned.

At that moment he could not have agreed with her more.

TWENTY-FOUR

The next morning Clint woke with Melanie's weight on his right arm. As quickly as he could without waking her he pulled his arm free, flexing his fingers to make sure his hand wasn't asleep.

"What's wrong?" she asked sleepily.

"Once, years ago, I woke up with my hand asleep," he said. "At that moment three men kicked in my door and came in shooting. Since then I make sure it never happens again."

"What happened?"

He looked at her.

"To the three men?"

"I killed them."

"Left-handed?" she asked.

He nodded.

"But I wouldn't want my life to depend on my left hand."

She rolled over him so that she was on his left side, then snuggled up against him.

"This better?" she asked.

"Much."

In another room in another part of town Helen Kramer was putting a plate of eggs in front of Woodrow Carver.

"Thank you, Helen."

She refilled his coffee cup, then sat down across from him with her own breakfast.

"Woodrow," she said, "I've never questioned you before, but . . ."

"Go ahead, Helen," he said. "If you can't question me, who can?"

"Why do you have to do it?"

"Do what?"

"Whatever it is you're going to do for my boss," she said.

"He's paying me."

"You don't need his money."

"Yeah, Helen, I do."

"But—"

"Look," he said, "I do what I do, Helen. I can't apologize to you for that."

"I know it, but—"

"I ain't one of those gentlemen you're used to."

"I'm glad you're not."

"But I've got to make my money the only way I know how," he went on. "Your boss has got somebody he wants killed. Have you ever heard of Clint Adams?"

"Clint Adams? You mean . . . the Gunsmith?"

"Yes."

"That's who he wants you to kill?"

"Yeah."

"But . . . you can't," she said. "He'll kill you."

"Not if I kill him first."

"Well . . . when are you supposed to do that?"

"I don't know," Carver said. "It seems to me he's tryin' to play with Adams's head a little first. But he'll tell me when he wants it done."

"And you'll do it?"

"Oh, yeah, I'll do it," he said. "Killin' the Gunsmith is gonna make me a lot of money."

"Enough for you to . . . stop what you're doing?" she asked.

He hesitated a moment, then said, "Maybe."

"Can you do it? I mean . . . alone?"

"I don't know," he said. "I might have to bring somebody else in. Somebody I work with a lot."

She fell silent. He reached across the table and took her hand.

"Don't worry, Helen," he said. "Everything's gonna be all right."

"I hope so, Woodrow," she said, squeezing his hand. "I hope so."

TWENTY-FIVE

Clint and Melanie had breakfast in the Denver House dining room. She further surprised him by not caring that she was wearing the same clothes as she had on the day before. She still managed to look neat and lovely.

"I'll go home and change before I go to work, though," she added at breakfast.

"I should warn you that Roper knows about us."

"You told him?"

"No, he guessed."

"Well . . . what does he know?"

"Not what we did last night," he said, "just that we had a meal together, but . . ."

"But he'll expect us to do what we did last night?" she asked.

"Yes."

"Well . . . I never was a very good liar," she said. "And keeping things from someone, that's the same as lying to me."

"Well, you don't have to talk about it," he said, "but you don't have to keep it from him, either."

"That will be a relief," she said. "I felt like I was walking on eggshells."

When they finished their breakfast, he walked her out to the front and had the doorman get a cab for her. She pecked his cheek and said, "Be careful."

"I'm always careful," he told her, helping her up into the cab.

From across the street Woodrow Carver watched Clint Adams help the woman into the cab. The driver snapped the reins at his horse and that left Adams standing there on the street, an easy target if Carver had wanted him today.

He studied the man as he stood there, then watched as he turned and started back inside. At that point there was a shot, and a bullet shattered some glass near Clint Adams's head.

Clint heard the glass shatter before he heard the shot, but he was tired of being shot at. And a split second earlier, Melanie might have been hurt.

So instead of ducking for cover, Clint turned and rushed headlong across the street. This was to surprise the shooter if not unnerve him. And it would certainly unnerve *her* if it was Laura who was shooting at him.

He made it to the other side of the street before another shot could be fired. He could see three doorways, which were empty. The shot had most likely come from a second- or third-story window, or a rooftop.

Clint made a decision, picked the building that he would have been most likely to use, and ran to find an open door. There was a store of some kind on the first floor, but next to it was another door. He opened it and found a stairway going up. He ran up to the second floor, then the third, which, in this building, was the top level. From there he tried to find a hatch to the roof, which he assumed—and hoped—would be in the hallway.

It was, and it was closed. He looked around, found a wooden chair, and used it to step up, lift the hatch off, and pull himself onto the roof.

Clint knew that this didn't necessarily have to be the correct roof, because once he was up there he had access to most of the other rooftops, since this one was the highest.

He looked both ways, hoping to see someone with a rifle, maybe running, but no one was in sight. He ran to the back of the roof and looked down. Whoever it was, he didn't know how they'd gotten off the roof so fast—unless they'd never been up there in the first place. If they'd shot at him from a window, then he made the wrong choice.

He took a walk to the adjoining rooftops, just to have a look around, maybe find the spent shell, but there was nothing.

He finally gave up and quit the roof. He replaced the hatch and the chair, and went back down to the street level. Instead of going back out the door he'd used to come in, he turned and looked for a back door. When he found it and used it, he found himself all alone in the back alley. He walked the length of it, looking up at the back of the buildings as he went. If the shooter had used a window, he could still be inside

one of the buildings, but there was no way he could
cover the front and the back. The shooter might be
hotfooting it out the front door even at that moment.

Clint decided that, whoever it was, they'd gotten
away.

Woodrow Carver pulled back into his doorway as
Clint Adams charged across the street. He waited until
Adams had gone inside, then stepped out. He looked
both ways, then stepped back. He decided to wait and
see who came out, Clint Adams or the shooter.

Carver watched as some people came out of the
hotel and started looking around, including the doorman. Some of them pointed, but he knew they didn't
know what they were pointing at.

Carver remained close to the building just in case
Clint Adams looked down on the street. He didn't want
to be spotted and mistaken for the shooter.

Finally, as he continued to wait, someone came
out of one of the buildings on his side of the street. It
was a girl carrying a rifle. She looked up quickly, then
both ways, then turned left and ran. Across the street
several people pointed at her and shouted.

Carver exited his doorway and headed left, decid-
ing to follow the girl to see where she would lead him.

TWENTY-SIX

When Clint came back across the street to the hotel, there was no shortage of people who were willing to talk to him. However, the descriptions he managed to get from them would have led him to believe that five shooters came running out of the building across the street.

He decided to depend more on the observations of the doorman than any of the other people.

"It was a woman," the doorman said to him, "a girl, really, who came out of that center building. I would have thought she was just scared the way she took off running down the block, but she was carrying a rifle."

"Did you see anyone else?"

"Like who?"

"I don't know," Clint said. "I'm just trying to figure this out. Was there anyone else across the street?"

"Well, there was a man standing in a doorway all morning," he said. "I figured he was probably waitin' for somebody."

"Like who?"

"Like a woman, maybe."

"And where is he now?" Clint asked.

"He's gone."

"When did he leave?"

"Well . . . he left right after that girl ran off," the doorman said, rubbing his jaw. "In fact, he went in the same direction."

"Okay . . . What's your name?"

"Ed."

"Ed, this is important."

"You want me to describe the girl?"

"No," Clint said. "I want you to describe the man in as much detail as you can."

"The man?" the doorman asked, confused. "But surely it was the girl who shot at you."

"You're probably right, Ed," Clint said, "but I still need to hear about the man. You see lots of people all day long, I'm sure you're very observant."

"Well, I am, kinda—"

"Good," Clint said. "Then help me to see this man in my mind, Ed. Tell me what he looked like."

TWENTY-SEVEN

Clint got to Talbot Roper's office before Melanie made it there. The outer office was empty, but when he knocked on Roper's door the detective yelled, "Come in!"

As Clint entered, Roper looked up and grinned.

"You again so soon?"

"I've got something for you," Clint said, "A description."

"Let's hear it."

Clint told Roper about the man the doorman at the Denver House had seen.

"That's a helluva description," Roper said. "Almost like a picture."

"Yeah, but the point is, do you know who it is?" Clint asked.

"No, but I can find out. Why don't you ask your buddy Sid Black?"

"I'm going to," Clint said. "Going there right after I leave here."

"Well, between us we'll probably be able to figure

out who he is," Roper said. "Now tell me what he did."

Clint told Roper about the shot that morning.

"Again? What happened?"

"I tried to catch her, but I made the wrong decision," Clint said. He told the detective about his running around on rooftops.

"While I was checking the back, she went out the front," Clint said. "According to the doorman, this guy followed her."

"You think he was working with her?" Roper asked.

"Maybe," Clint said. "Or maybe she's in trouble."

"She's in— She's tryin' to kill you, Clint!" Roper said. "Why would you worry if she's in trouble? Maybe this guy will take care of her for you."

"I don't want her taken care of, Tal," Clint said. "She's a kid, a mixed-up kid. I want to keep her from getting killed."

Roper stood up.

"You're not blamin' yourself for her sister getting killed, are you?"

"Not exactly."

"But you're feelin' some guilt," Roper said. "I know you, Clint."

"Yeah, okay, some," Clint said. "Enough."

"Okay, go talk to Black. I'll circulate the description. We'll come up with the name and we'll find him. Then if he knows where she is, we'll get it out of him."

"Thanks, Tal," Clint said. "I'll owe you."

"Yeah, you will."

* * *

Clint left Roper's before Melanie got there and headed over to Sid Black's place. For some reason the front door was open, so he walked in. The bartender, Boris, was behind the bar, polishing the wood.

"Hey, Mr. Adams," he greeted happily.

"Hey, Boris," Clint said. "Front doors were open."

"Yeah, but we're still closed. I was just airin' the place out. You want a beer?"

"Sure. Sid around?"

"Naw, he's out. Only reason I got the doors open. He don't like when I do it."

He put a beer in front of Clint.

"Why do you do it, then?"

"'Cause if I didn't, this place would smell like a barn."

"Doesn't Sid notice?"

"Sid grew up in a barn," Boris said. "He don't notice nothin'."

Clint took a sip of the beer. It was ice cold and good.

"Why'd ya wanna see Sid so early?" Boris asked.

"I'm looking for a guy," Clint said. "I thought Sid might know him."

"Who's that?"

"I don't know his name," Clint said. "All I've got is a description."

"Let me hear it," Boris said, leaning on the bar. "I know most of the people Sid knows."

Clint gave Boris the full description the doorman gave him.

"Big jug ears?" Boris asked.

"That's what the doorman said," Clint replied. "He could see them from across the street. If you give Sid the description, maybe he can—"

"You don't need Sid," Boris said. "That's Woodrow Carver."

"Carver? I never heard of him."

"He's a gunhand," Boris said. "Local, which is probably why you ain't heard of him."

"Gun for hire?"

"Sure," Boris said.

"Who's he work for?"

"Anybody with money."

"Who's he working for now?"

"Well," Boris said, "for that maybe you do need Sid. When he gets back, I'll ask him."

"How do you know who Carver is?" Clint asked.

"That's easy," Boris said, straightening. "He comes in here."

"When?"

"Most nights."

"Boris, you were right."

"About what?"

Clint reached out and slapped the bartender on the shoulder.

"I didn't need Sid after all."

"Well, you'll probably need him to find out who Carver's workin' for."

"Maybe not."

"Whataya mean?"

"I mean I'll be here tonight and when Mr. Carver shows up, I'll just ask him myself."

Boris grinned.

"That I gotta see."

Clint went straight back to Roper's office. Melanie was there this time and smiled when he came in.

"He told me you'd just left when I got here," she said. "What's going on?"

"I just need to talk to him again for a minute."

"Sure, Clint," she said. "Go ahead in."

Clint knocked and entered.

"Find out somethin' already?"

Clint told him about Woodrow Carver.

"Yeah, I know the name," Roper said. "He's a gun for hire, not in your league, or anybody else's, for that matter. He won't come at you alone if it's him. You better watch your back."

"Why don't you watch it for me?" Clint said. "I'm going back to the Arcade tonight. Boris the bartender told me Carver comes in there all the time."

"Well, okay then," Roper said. "We'll go over there together and see what this guy knows. Meanwhile, let me see if I can find out who he's workin' for."

"What for? When we see him we'll ask him."

"Yeah, but this way we'll know if he's lying."

TWENTY-EIGHT

Carver had followed the girl to a hotel down by the docks. He let her go in alone, then followed soon after. She had already gone up the stairs.

"The girl that just came in," he said, approaching the bored-looking desk clerk.

"What about her?"

"What's her name?"

"How do I know?"

"Well, what room is she in?"

"I don't know—"

Carver took out his gun and placed the barrel under the man's nose.

"Try to think."

The clerk gulped, turned the desk register around, and pointed.

"That's her."

Carver looked at the name: Laura Kellogg.

"That's what I thought."

He removed the gun barrel from the clerk's face. The man heaved a sigh of relief.

"She have a man up there with her a lot?"

The clerk nodded. "Fella named Wilson."

Carver nodded, said, "Thanks for the information."

He left the hotel and headed for the bank.

"She did what?" the banker asked.

"She took a shot at Adams," Carver said. "I thought you had her and her boyfriend under control."

Wilson wasn't the girl's boyfriend, but the banker let that go.

"Are you sure it was her?"

"I followed her back to her hotel, checked the register, talked to the desk clerk," Carver said. "It was her."

The banker frowned.

"I got a good mind to take care of her first," Carver complained. "If she manages to kill Adams, it's gonna cost me money."

The banker stared at Carver, then said, "I'm sorry, I was just—you said if you had a good mind. I just find that . . ."

Carver knew he was being insulted. He wondered how much money the banker had in his wallet now, and if it would be worth killing him for it.

"I'm just tellin' you," Carver said, "you don't got things as under control as you think."

"Well, don't worry," the banker said. "I will. Don't you worry. Just go out tonight and do whatever it is you do to relax. We'll talk in the morning."

Carver pointed his finger at the banker.

"I won't stand for anybody costin' me money," he said. "I'll kill both of them first."

"I understand," the banker said, "and that might not be a bad idea . . . but I'll let you know."

Carver was so worked up he didn't stop to talk to Helen Kramer on the way out.

The banker had not been a happy man to begin with, not after what had happened between him and Rita. He had sent her dozens of roses to try to get back into her good graces. If he had to depend on his wife for sex, he might end up trying to go back to his secretary, Helen. She still looked pretty good for her age.

However, now that Carver was gone, he was livid, not so much at the girl as at Dirk Wilson, who was supposed to be controlling her.

Carver might have been right. It might be better to get rid of the girl and Wilson, pin both those killings on the Gunsmith, too.

All he needed was for Woodrow Carver to keep out of trouble.

Outside on the street Carver thought he probably should have killed Wilson and the girl before he went to see the banker. Then the man would have had no choice but to let him go after Clint Adams.

He decided to take the banker's advice, though. He was going to go where he was able to relax, and at the same time he'd line up the men he was going to use to back his play against the Gunsmith.

Dave Mello and Albert Nunez both liked watching the dancing girls at Sid Black's Arcade, and both were fair to good hands with a gun. Tonight he'd sign them

up to back his play, promise them a small portion of
what he was getting paid, plus a shot at the Gunsmith.

It was only after he'd walked three blocks that he
realized he hadn't said a word to Helen.

TWENTY-NINE

Clint and Roper were standing at the bar in the Arcade when Sid Black came walking over.

"Heard you were lookin' for Woodrow Carver," he said to Clint.

"That's right."

"He ain't here yet, but he comes in most nights. You gonna kill 'im?"

"I just want to talk to him," Clint said.

"So you're not gonna shoot my place up?" Sid asked.

"Not if I can help it," Clint said. "I guess it'll be up to Carver."

"When he comes in, does he usually come in alone?" Roper asked.

"Sometimes yes, sometimes no," Black said. "Sometimes he comes in with a couple of guys."

"Men in the same business?" Clint asked.

"Pretty much."

"You know who Carver works for?" Clint asked.

"Usually anybody with money."

"Anybody in particular now?" Roper asked.

"I heard he's doin' some work for some banker," Black said, "but I don't have a name."

"We can get that from Carver, himself," Clint said to Roper.

"You really think you're gonna get him to talk?" Sid Black asked.

"Yes, I do."

"Shit," Black said.

"What?" Roper asked.

"Damage," Black said. "I see damage to my place comin'."

"Like we said," Clint responded, "it'll be up to him."

Sid Black walked away, shaking his head and muttering, "Damage . . ."

Dave Mello and Al Nunez were already in the Arcade, watching the dancing girls and waiting for Woodrow Carver to arrive. They paid no attention to the two men at the bar, although if they had, they might have recognized Talbot Roper, who was fairly well-known in Denver on both sides of the law.

They did, however, notice when Carver entered the place, and they weren't the only ones.

Boris came over to where Clint and Roper were standing and said, "Carver just came in."

They both turned their heads and saw the man who had just entered. He stopped just inside the doors, looked around, then strode across the room to a table where two men were seated.

"Who are they?" Clint asked Boris. "Some of those friends you say he comes here with?"

"They look familiar, but I got no names comin' to mind."

"Okay," Clint said.

"How do you want to play this?" Roper asked.

"I'll go over there alone, you cover me from here."

"That may be hard," Roper said. "This place is pretty full."

"Do the best you can."

"Thanks."

"I just want to talk to him," Clint said. "Probably nothing will happen."

"Yeah," Roper said, "probably."

THIRTY

Clint left his beer on the bar so both his hands would be free as he approached the table of three men.

Woodrow Carver looked up at him as he got nearer, and Clint saw recognition in the man's eyes. Why not? He'd been standing across the street from the Denver House hotel.

"Woodrow Carver?" he asked.

"Who wants to know?" the big-eared man asked.

"Don't play games, Carver," Clint said. "You know who I am."

"And you probably know who I am, so what are ya askin' for?" the man replied.

"Fine," Clint said, "then none of us will play games. Who are your friends?"

"None of yer business," Carver said. "What do you want, Adams?"

"I want to know who you're working for, Carver," Clint said. "Who's paying the freight right now?"

"Why should I tell you that?" the man asked.

The other two men were looking nervous. Clint

was thinking they must have been caught by surprise when they heard who he was, and now they were wondering what was going on.

"Because I'm asking."

"Nice try," Carver said, "but it's none of your business who I'm workin' for. What else?"

"You were across the street from my hotel this morning when a girl took a shot at me."

Carver laughed.

"You got women shootin' at you now, Adams?" he asked. "That's rich."

"One woman in particular," Clint said, "and I'd like to find her."

"What makes you think I can help?"

"You followed her this morning."

"Who says?"

"Witnesses."

"Your witnesses are wrong."

"I don't think so," Clint said. "I want to know where that girl is."

"What makes you think I'd tell you even if I knew?" Carver asked.

"I was hoping you'd just tell me because I asked nicely," Clint said.

"I think it's nice of the three of us to not just stand up and gun you, Adams," Carver said. "Sure would be a feather in our caps, eh, boys?"

Both of the other men's eyes got wider.

"I don't think your buddies here are ready for that, Carver," Clint said. "I don't think you filled them in on why you wanted them to meet you here." Clint looked at them. "You boys didn't know that he wanted you to take on the Gunsmith? Or back his play?"

Carver looked at his two friends, who seemed very nervous.

"W-we just came to look at some dancin' girls," Mello said.

"Yeah, and to drink some whiskey," Nunez added.

"See?" Clint said to Carver. "No help here."

Carver looked at Clint, and then past him.

"Ah, you spotted my friend Roper," Clint said. "See? I do have willing backup."

Carver looked up at Clint. He had his gun hand around his beer mug, and flexed it. Clint was sure he wanted to toss that beer into his face, and then go for his gun. But he was just as sure the man wouldn't do it.

"Why don't you give my requests some thought," Clint said. "I'm going to go back to the bar and finish my beer."

Clint knew he was taking a chance—even with Roper watching—but he turned his back on the three men and walked nonchalantly back to the bar.

THIRTY-ONE

"How'd it go?" Roper asked.

"I think he was recruiting those two to back his play," Clint said, "but we barged in too soon."

"So how'd you leave it?"

"I gave him some time to think things over," Clint said.

"Nobody's gonna start shootin'?" Boris asked.

"He knows Roper's here, too," Clint said. "He's not going to try anything."

Clint noticed that Boris had his hands beneath the bar.

"You can take your hands off that scattergun, Boris," Clint said.

Boris brought his hands out and laced them on top of the bar.

"Just doin' my job, Mr. Adams," Boris said. "The boss told me to watch out for things."

"That's okay, Boris," Clint said. "We can watch out for things."

"Okay," Boris said, "whatever you say." He went

to the other end of the bar to serve some other customers.

"He's not gonna talk," Roper said. "What do you want to do?"

"He knows where the girl is," Clint said. "If he's not going to talk, we're going to make him talk."

"Isn't it more important to find out who he's workin' for?" Roper asked. "Who wants you dead?"

"Later," Clint said. "We've got to find that girl and help her."

"Even though she wants to kill you?"

"I didn't kill her father, or her sister," Clint said. "I'll convince her of that."

"I hope you're persuasive."

"With him," Clint asked, "or with her?"

"You two were no damn help," Carver complained.

"Yeah, well," Mello said, "you didn't say nothin' about no Gunsmith."

"You must be crazy thinkin' we'd go against Adams," Nunez said.

"Three against one, we coulda took him," Carver said.

"Three against two," Mello said. "I shoulda seen it before, but that's Talbot Roper at the bar. I wouldn't go against either one of them with only three-to-one odds. I'm leavin'."

"Me, too," Nunez said.

"Wait, wait—" Carver said, but the two men got up and left quickly.

Carver had to quell the urge to run, looked over at

the bar, and saw Clint Adams and Talbot Roper watching him.

His mind raced, trying to come up with an idea of what to do.

"Well, he's alone now," Roper said.

"He was alone before, too," Clint said. "It's just that now they actually walked out."

"Look at him," Roper said. "He's ready to run."

"If he does, we'll chase him."

"We'll have to," Roper said. "We won't be able to follow him."

"Too bad we couldn't—" Clint stopped short.

"What?"

"Following him would be the best thing to do," Clint decided.

"But we can't," Roper said. "He knows both of us."

"Don't you have somebody you can use for that?" Clint asked.

"Yes, but I don't think I could get him here in time to follow him tonight."

"And we need to do it tonight," Clint said, "or we might lose him."

"You don't want to try to force him to talk?"

"We might end up killing him. I have a better idea."

Clint waved at Boris to come over.

"Two more?"

"We need some help, Boris," Clint said. "Either you can help us, or I can ask Sid."

"What do you need?"

"Somebody reliable," Clint said, "to follow some-body."

"Just to follow? Nothing else?"

"Nothing else."

"I've got just the little weas— I mean, just the man. He'll be cheap."

"Just get to him quick and tell him I want him to follow Carver."

"Okay."

"Does this little weas— Uh, this man know Carver?"

"He knows who he is, but Carver won't know him, if that's what you're worried about."

"That's what I'm worried about."

"How long do you want him to follow him?" Boris asked.

"Tonight, and tomorrow morning. Tell him to come to the Denver House hotel and meet me in the lobby at noon with his information."

"Okay."

"How much will he be?"

Boris told him and Clint handed over the money.

"Tell him I'll give him that much again if he's not late tomorrow."

"But I can get him for you so cheap."

"I'll give you the same amount."

"Sold," Boris said.

"What's the man's name?"

"Floyd," Boris said. "Floyd Hannah."

"And does he look like a weasel?"

"Exactly like a weasel," Boris said with a laugh.

"You won't be able to miss him, not in the lobby of the Denver House."

"Okay, then," Clint said. "Go and recruit him."

"Yes, sir."

"So what do we do now?" Roper asked.

"Let's have another beer."

THIRTY-TWO

Carver finally decided to make his move. He was just going to get up and walk out. If they followed him out, he'd have no choice but to go for his gun. But if Adams wanted answers to his questions, he couldn't afford to kill him.

He was going to take the chance.

He stood up and headed for the door.

"There he goes," Roper said. "Still want to let him go?"

"Yes," Clint said.

"Okay," Roper said. "It's your funeral."

Clint knew he'd taken a big chance trusting a man he didn't know, had never met, but he also didn't want to take the chance that he'd have to kill Woodrow Carver before he could get the man to talk. So maybe he'd be able to get the answers he needed just by having the man followed.

There were two immediate questions. Where was

Laura Kellogg? And who was Carver working for?
There were other questions, as well, but they could
wait until later. These two main ones had to be answered.

Clint went back to the hotel, telling Roper he
could go home for the night.

"I'll stay inside so I won't be needing anybody to
watch my back," Clint promised.

"What about tomorrow at noon?"

"I don't think I'll be needing any help with Floyd
the weasel," Clint told him.

So Roper went home, and Clint back to the Denver
House. When he got to his room he half expected to
find Melanie there, but when he found the room empty
he wasn't all that disappointed. He figured he needed
a good night's sleep. Maybe the next day would bring
him the answers he needed.

Carver checked his trail on the way home from the
saloon, but he didn't spot either Clint Adams or Talbot Roper. They had let him go pretty easily and he
couldn't figure out why. He checked out his window
from time to time, but he didn't see anyone. He decided to go to bed, get up early, and go see the banker.

Floyd Hannah stood outside Woodrow Carver's hotel
and watched the light in the man's window go out. He
knew the man had been checking behind him to see if
he was being followed, but for the money he was being paid the weasel made sure he wasn't spotted.

Since he also had to follow Carver in the morning,
he found himself a nice comfortable doorway, curled

up in it, and went to sleep. He knew he'd wake up at first light. He always did.

He wished he had a bottle of whiskey to curl up with, but he wouldn't take a drink until after his job was done. He wasn't about to endanger the second part of his payment.

Clint could still smell Melanie on his sheets. He supposed she had stayed away because he'd been inattentive at the office that morning. He'd apologize when he saw her next time.

He got up and walked to the window. He couldn't see anything across the street, and he'd kept it dark in the room so nobody could see him.

He hoped the weasel was as good at following people as Boris seemed to think he was.

THIRTY-THREE

As always, Floyd woke with the first showing of the sun. He rubbed his eyes, trying to clear them. He wished he had time for some breakfast or a drink. By the time Woodrow Carver came out the front door of his hotel, Floyd's eyes were clear.

He followed Carver to two different addresses, and then went to meet Clint Adams in the lobby of the Denver House hotel at noon.

Clint was impressed when a weasely looking man entered the hotel lobby at five minutes to noon.

"You Floyd?" he asked as the man passed near him.

The man stopped short and looked Clint up and down.

"Adams?"

"That's right."

"You got the rest of my money for me?"

"You got information for me?"

"What about some breakfast?" the man asked.

Clint did not want to eat breakfast across the table

from a man who looked as much like a weasel as this man did. Boris had not been exaggerating.

"I'm not going to buy you breakfast, Floyd," Clint said. "Buy it yourself after I pay you. Now come on. What have you got for me?"

Floyd hesitated, then gave Clint the two addresses he'd tailed Carver to.

"He went into the first place for about five minutes, but he was in the bank for almost twenty."

"And the first place was a hotel?"

Floyd nodded.

"A run-down fleabag down by the docks."

"Okay," Clint said. He took out the rest of the little man's money and gave it to him.

"Much obliged, Mr. Gunsmith," Floyd said. "You need me ta do anythin' else, just talk ta Boris."

"Yeah, I'll do that, Floyd. Thanks."

Clint wondered if Floyd was going to try to get into the Denver House dining room for breakfast, but the man went right to the front door and left the hotel.

Armed with both addresses, Clint went outside and had the doorman get him a cab.

He stood outside the fleabag hotel, staring up at it, then went into the lobby. The desk clerk saw him coming and reacted nervously.

"Can I help ya?"

"I'm looking for a girl."

"We don't do that here."

"No. I mean, I'm looking for one of your guests."

Hastily, the man turned the register book around and pushed it toward Clint.

"Thanks."

He read the names on the page, saw Laura Kellogg right away. She was in room 5.

"Thanks," he said again, and headed for the stairs to the second floor.

"Um, you ain't gonna do no shootin', are ya?" the clerk called out.

Why was everybody asking him that?

"No," he said. "I don't intend to do any shooting."

He ignored the clerk and walked up to the second floor.

He walked along the hallway until he came to room 5, then stopped and knocked.

"Did you forget your key—" Laura Kellogg asked as she opened the door. She stopped short when she saw Clint, then turned and ran back into the room. Clint figured she was going for her gun, so he went after her and caught her before she could grab her rifle.

"Let me go!" she yelled. "You murderer! Let me go. I'll kill you!"

"You've tried enough times and missed, Laura," he said, holding her wrists. "Now settle down."

"I'll kill you, I'll kill you—"

He pushed her down on the bed, got on top of her, and straddled her, holding her arms down.

"Go ahead," she said, "rape me. You're a murderer, you're probably a rapist, too."

"I'm not a rapist or a murderer," he said. "And if you'll calm down, I'll try to convince you of that."

She bucked for a few seconds more, then went limp.

"All right," she said. "I'm calm. Get off me."

He climbed off her and stood up. She rolled over

and quickly reached for her rifle, but he snatched it up and then stepped away from her.

"What do you want, Adams?" she demanded. "You want to finish off my family for good?"

"Look, you little idiot!" he said. "I'm trying to tell you I didn't kill anyone in your family."

"If you didn't kill my sister, then who did?"

"I don't know," he said, "but I'm trying to find out. Only looking for you has kept me from getting it done."

"Why would you want to find out who killed her?" she demanded.

"Because she came to me for help, and before I could help her she was dead."

"Help? What kind of help did she want from you?"

"Well, for one thing she wanted me to find you," he said, "and keep you from becoming a murderer."

"Why you?"

"I guess she figured you were trying to kill me, so maybe I could stop you."

"And kill me?"

"You really think your poor sister wanted me to kill you, Laura? She loved you, and wanted to keep you from becoming a killer. And she also didn't want you getting killed."

Laura straightened herself out and sat on the side of the bed, her hands in her lap. Her head was bowed and it took a moment for Clint to realize she was crying silently. From the slump of her shoulders he could see that the fight had gone out of her.

THIRTY-FOUR

"You asked me who killed your sister if I didn't," Clint said. "Do you know a man named Woodrow Carver?"

She wiped the tears from her face with the heels of her hands and said, "No, I don't."

"Well, somebody's been helping you, right?"

She hesitated.

"Laura, if I wanted you dead I would have killed you by now, right? What's to stop me?"

After a moment she said, "Yes, someone's helping me."

"What's his name?"

"Wilson. Dirk Wilson."

Clint didn't know the name.

"Why is he helping you?"

"I think . . . He wants me to be his girl."

She sounded terribly naïve.

"Does he have a boss?" Clint asked. "Somebody he's working for? Somebody who's telling him what to do?"

She looked up at Clint.

"I don't know," she said. "Sometimes he says things that . . . make me think so, but . . . why would someone be telling him to help me?"

"I don't know," Clint said. "That's what I'm trying to find out. Where did you meet Wilson?"

"Here, in Denver."

"You mean recently. But . . . hasn't he been helping you for months?"

"Yes, he has," she said. "We met when I first came West. I came right to Denver, because I heard you came here a lot."

"And did you meet him right away?"

"No, it took a few days."

"And where did you meet?"

"In a saloon."

"What were you doing there?"

"Actually, I was looking for someone to help me, to guide me. I mean, not really tell me what to do but to guide me geographically. He must have heard I was looking and . . ."

"And what?"

"He offered his services."

"For how much?"

"Free," she said.

"Didn't you find that odd?"

"Well . . . I guess I should have." She stood up suddenly. "You think I'm being manipulated?"

"I do."

"By Dirk?"

"No, it's got to be someone behind him, someone Woodrow Carver is working for."

"And who's Carver?"

"A gunman."

"Well, Dirk is no gunman. He's a tracker, and a good one."

Clint could believe that. All the times that Laura had taken a shot at him he hadn't seen her coming. Now he knew why.

"Laura, there's a bank in town called First Priority. Do you have anything to do with it?"

"Well, yes," she said. "I opened an account there when I first came here."

"How much money did you put in?"

"Thousands, and I've transferred more in as we've needed it."

"So your family is wealthy?"

"What's left of it."

Suddenly, she sank back down on the bed, reminded that she really didn't have that much family left.

"Look, Laura . . . I liked your sister, and I wanted to help both of you. Will you let me help you?"

"Help me what?" she asked. "My only goal was to kill you. Without that . . . I've got nothing."

"Let me help you find a new goal."

"Why?" She looked up at him. "Why do you want to help me? For money?"

"No, not for money."

"Well, you don't want me, so what is it then?"

"Maybe it's . . . guilt."

"Guilt?" she asked. "But you said—"

"I didn't kill your sister," he said, "and I didn't kill your father all those years ago, but . . . I didn't save him, either."

"Could you have?"

"Maybe," he said. "Maybe I could have. See . . . This may be hard for you to hear."

"Oh, please," she said. "Please. All these years, if I haven't heard the truth I'd like to hear it now."

"Are you sure?"

"Yes."

"All right," he said, sitting on the bed, but leaving space between them, "then I'll tell you a story."

THIRTY-FIVE

About twenty years earlier

Bisbee, Arizona

The Lucky Lady was alive with activity when Clint Adams walked in. The piano player in the corner was pounding away, girls were working the floor, and all the gaming tables were going strong. Faro and poker tables were especially busy.

Clint walked to the bar and ordered a beer. When he had it in his hand, he turned his back to the bar and leaned against it. One poker table in particular caught his eye, mainly because one man in particular had stacks of chips in front of him. Not only was he winning, but he was gloating, lording it over the other four players.

"Yes, sir," the man with all the chips said, "you boys sure made a mistake when you let me sit down at your table. I'm about as hot as I can be."

"Shut up," one of the men said. "Just shut up and deal."

It only took a few hands for Clint to see why the man was so hot—he was cheating. And not only when it was his deal. He was good at it, too, but not so good that he wouldn't get caught.

In fact, Clint could see two of the other players watching him carefully as the deal came back around to him. Yup, the man was good at it, but he was doing it too often. He should have kept the cheating to a minimum, maybe one good hand an hour. And he never should have gloated.

Finally, they had him. The two men stood up quickly and drew their guns.

"Yer cheatin'!" one of them yelled. He was a tall man with sandy-colored hair and a brown mole on the point of his chin.

"Took them this long to figure that out?" the bartender said from behind Clint.

The cheater, who looked like a drummer, sat back in his chair and spread his hands. The other players got up and left so fast they knocked over their chairs. The piano stopped and all attention fell on the three men.

"What do you mean?"

"Yer cheatin', and lordin' it over us," the second man said.

Clint couldn't believe that the cheater wasn't smart enough to deny it.

"Now come on, fellows," the man said, laughing. "It was all in fun. Tell you what, I'll just give you your money back."

"That ain't the way it works in the West, friend," the first man said.

"You all heard 'im," the second man said. "He ain't denyin' it."

"B-but it's just cards," the cheat said.

"It's poker, friend," the first man said. "And we take our poker real serious."

The second man cocked the hammer on his gun.

"They're gonna kill 'im," the bartender said.

"Looks like it," Clint said.

"Ain't you gonna do somethin'?"

"Why should I?"

"You're the Gunsmith, ain'tcha?"

"So? Don't you have a lawman here in town?"

"Yeah, but—"

"Send somebody for him."

"It'll be too late."

"Well, you've got a shotgun under the bar, don't you?" Clint asked.

"Yeah, but—"

"So *you* do something."

"I ain't a gunman," the bartender said. "You are."

"And whatever happens here," Clint said, "whoever gets shot, I'm going to get the blame just because I'm here." Clint turned and looked at the man. "You're my witness to the fact that I didn't do a thing."

At that point he heard two shots.

Later, in the sheriff's office, the lawman gave Clint back his gun and holster.

"Okay," he said, "you're free to go."

"The bartender backed my story?"

"Yep," the sheriff replied. "Says you coulda saved that drummer's life, but you decided to do nothin'."

"It wasn't my job, Sheriff," Clint said. "That was your job."

"Did you use to be a lawman, Adams?"

"Once upon a time."

"Seems to me this sorta thing would always be your job, badge or not."

Clint strapped on his gun. He didn't say anything to the lawman, but the time he'd been sitting in a cell while the sheriff checked his story he'd started thinking the same thing. What would it have cost him to save the hapless poker cheat's life? He probably had a family somewhere back East.

"Sheriff, what was his name?"

"Who?"

"The poker cheat."

"I don't know," the lawman said, "Kellogg . . . yeah, that was it, Kellogg."

Kellogg . . .

"After that," he told Laura, "I started stepping in when trouble was developing right in front of me."

"So," she said quietly, "you didn't kill him, but you didn't help him, either."

"I guess you could say that."

"And if I want to kill you for that," she went on, "I'd have to kill everybody in that saloon."

"I guess that's one way of looking at it."

"And what happened to the two men who did kill him?" she asked.

"I don't know," Clint said. "I think they left the

saloon before the sheriff got there, and while the sheriff was busy trying to blame me, they left town."

"And they were never caught?"

"I don't think so."

"But you don't know for sure."

"No," he said. "I left town the day the sheriff let me go."

They both fell quiet for a while. Clint had never felt sorrier for not helping Kellogg than he did right at that moment.

"Thomas," she said then.

"What?"

"My father's name," she said. "It was Tom Kellogg."

THIRTY-SIX

"So my father was a card cheat," she said glumly.

"I don't know if he ever cheated before that," he said. "He seemed to take it a lot more lightly than the others at the table. I don't think he thought it was that big a deal, not being from the West."

"Why would my mother tell me you killed him?"

"I was there," Clint said. "In town, in that saloon. Word got around. Even back then when somebody got killed and I was around, people tended to put two and two together and come up with the wrong answer."

"I don't know what to believe."

"Can you believe that this Dirk Wilson is helping you just out of the goodness of his heart?" he asked.

"I suppose I would be naïve to believe that," she admitted.

"Laura," Clint said, "if I was the killer you think I am, you'd be dead."

"I suppose . . ."

"I know it's hard to give up something you've

believed most of your life," Clint said. "There's got to be some way I can convince you that I'm innocent."

She shook her head and said, "I don't know . . ."

Clint knew he was about to take a big chance, but he didn't think the girl had it in her. He walked over to her and held her rifle out to her.

"Here," he said, "if you're still convinced that I killed your father and your sister, take this and kill me now."

She stared at him, her eyes wide. She stood up and took the rifle from him. She'd taken many potshots at him from afar, but he didn't think she had it in her to shoot him up close. Not after all the talking he'd just done.

"Go ahead, Laura."

She clenched and unclenched her hands on her rifle, firmed her jaw, but suddenly she simply turned and dropped the rifle on the bed.

"No," she said.

"I didn't think so," he said. "Look, I've got one more stop to make."

"Where?"

"I think I know where to find who's behind this," he said. "I don't know who it is, but I have an address. Don't leave this room until I come back."

"But what if . . . What if Dirk comes back?" she asked.

"What's he been telling you?"

"To stay inside."

"Does he know you took a shot at me yesterday morning?" Clint asked.

"Yes."

"And?"

"He was very angry."

"Okay, then," Clint replied, "if he comes back, just tell him you're staying inside. And just stay right here until I come back."

Clint turned and headed for the door. He put his hand on the doorknob and turned back.

"I may have all the answers for both of us later today," he said.

"Well," she said, "you go and do what you have to do, Mr. Adams. I'll just . . . sit here and wait, and think about what you've told me."

"Good."

She lifted her head and looked at him.

"Maybe I'll come to the decision that you're still responsible, in some way. Maybe I'll decide that I have no other recourse than to try to kill you."

"Miss Kellogg," he said, "I sincerely hope you don't come to that decision."

THIRTY-SEVEN

Clint stopped just outside the First Priority Bank, a big white stone building that stood two stories high. Inside was a man who wanted him dead, a man who was willing to use two sisters and their family history to not only kill him but . . . what? Make him feel guilt? Frame him for murder?

He went inside and stepped up to one of the tellers' cages.

"Can I help you, sir?"

"Yes," Clint said. "Who's in charge?"

"Well, that'd be Mr. Wellington, our head teller. Shall I get him for you?"

"No," Clint said. "Who's in charge of the whole bank?"

"That'd be our bank manager, Mr. Holmstead."

Holmstead. That name didn't mean anything to him. Neither did Wellington.

"I'd like to see Mr. Holmstead," he said.

"And what's your name, sir?" the bow-tied teller

asked. He looked as if he'd been behind that window, those bars, for years.

"You tell him Clint Adams would like to see him."

"Well," the teller said, "you wait here and I'll go tell him."

There were five tellers' windows in the place, and a lot of desks off to the side. Clint had been in banks this size before, but only in New York and California.

The teller had come out from behind his cage and walked a long way to knock on a door and enter. Clint became aware that people were looking at him, watching him. Did they think he was robbing the bank? Hadn't anybody ever asked to see the bank manager before?

When the teller returned, he had an attractive, fifty-ish woman with him. She regarded Clint from behind wire-framed glasses.

"Mr. Adams?"

"Yes."

"Mr. Holmstead will see you now. Please follow me."

"Thank you."

He followed her to the doorway against the back wall. They entered an outer office where there was an empty desk he assumed was hers. She walked to a second door, knocked, opened it, and said, "You can go in, sir."

"Thank you," he said again, and entered.

As he walked in, she closed the door behind him. The man behind the desk stood. As soon as Clint saw him, he knew he had the right man. It had been twenty years, but he was still sandy-haired and he still had a brown mole on the point of his chin.

"I see you recognize me," the man said.

Clint looked around.

"Where's your friend?" he asked.

"My frie— Oh, the other player, you mean?"

"The other man who gunned Tom Kellogg down."

"Oh, well, he died years ago," Holmstead said. "Sit down, please."

Clint sat.

"I am not a great believer in coincidence," the banker said.

"Neither am I."

"But I am a believer in fate," he said. "I suppose it was fate that we all come together in the same place— you, me, and the daughters of the man I killed."

"I'm not all that sure I believe in fate, either," Clint said.

"Well, then, what would you call it?"

Clint shrugged and suggested, "Justice?"

THIRTY-EIGHT

"Justice?" the banker Holmstead said. "For a card cheat?"

"Is that what I meant?"

"Then what? Justice for you?"

Clint looked at the nameplate on the man's desk. Mr. Harold Holmstead.

"Harold," he said, "what's your connection with Laura Kellogg? Woodrow Carver? And Dirk Wilson?"

Clint could see the man was shaken by the knowledge he seemed to have, but he wasn't about to admit it.

"Am I supposed to know these people?"

"Shall I tell you what I think?" Clint said.

"Please do."

"I think both Carver and Wilson work for you," Clint said. "Whether they know about each other I'm not sure. But you somehow heard that Laura Kellogg was in Denver looking for her father's killer, and you thought that was you. You probably sent Wilson to find out for sure and he came back with the news that she wasn't looking for you for killing her father twenty years ago, but for me."

"Fascinating."

"So you decided to help her find me, and kill me, but not all at once. You decided to get me here, and then you were probably going to get rid of her and pin it on me, only her sister arrived."

"Do tell."

"Right. So you had her sister killed, tried to pin that one on me. But it didn't stick, so my guess is you still intend to have Laura Kellogg show up dead and pin it on me. Or, by now, you've considered that it would just be better for everyone if she and I were both dead."

"And you have worked this all out for yourself?" the banker asked.

"Pretty much."

"And shared your theory with the police?"

"Oh no," Clint said, "I thought I'd resolve this matter by myself."

The banker tensed.

"If you kill me now . . . Everyone saw you come in here."

"Oh, no, not here," Clint said, "and not now. No, no, at a time and place of my choosing. That was your plan all along, right? To have it done where and when you wanted? Well, now it's the other way around."

Clint stood up, walked to the door, then turned.

"I'll decide where and when," he said. "And I'll decide by who." He pointed a finger at the banker. "And whoever you send after me—Carver, Wilson—

I'll send back to you in a box. But it won't be long before you have a box of your own."

"You're crazy," the banker said. "You can't threaten me."

"You can still be arrested for murder, you know," Clint said. "That's been your biggest fear all these years, right? That somebody who saw you that day might show up, now that you're a man of position?"

"He was a goddamned card cheat," Holmstead said. "Nobody would blame me for what I did."

"His daughter would."

Clint opened the door.

"Why didn't you do something all those years ago?" the banker demanded. "If you'd stepped in, it never would have happened."

"I know it," Clint said. "Believe me, I've been thinking a lot about that these past few days, but you know what? I've decided that none of this was my fault. This is all your doing. It was *your* decision all those years ago that set us all on this path. And you know what? *You're* going to pay the price."

He went out the door and left it open.

Helen watched the man walk away. She'd heard the last few sentences he exchanged with her boss. So this was the man Woodrow was supposed to kill? The famous Clint Adams, the Gunsmith?

"Helen!"

She turned and entered her boss's office. He was seated behind his desk, his face drawn and pale.

"Get me Carver," he said. "Now."

"Yes, sir."

"And I'm not seeing anyone else today," he added. "Just Carver, or Wilson."

"Yes, sir."

"That's all."

She pulled his door closed, wondering how much easier this might be for all concerned if the Gunsmith had just killed him now.

THIRTY-NINE

Clint left the bank, satisfied that he'd found his man, and his answers. Now he needed to come up with some solutions.

First he needed to tell Talbot Roper everything that had happened, so he headed right to the detective's office.

When he entered, Melanie looked up at him, her face expressionless.

"He's been expecting you," she said. "Go ahead in."

"Melanie—"

"I'm sorry, I have work to do."

He decided not to press her. Maybe she'd come around later and he'd be able to apologize.

He entered Roper's office.

"Expecting me?" Clint asked.

"All the time, now," Roper said. "I've got some good news."

"What?"

"I've found your girl. She's in a hotel down by the docks—"

"I know," Clint said. "I was there this morning."

"Your weasel came through?"

"Yes."

"And you talked to her?"

"Yes," Clint said.

"So you know what's goin' on?"

"I do."

"And you're gonna tell me?"

"Have a seat," Clint said, "and I'll tell you the whole story."

"Well," Roper said when Clint was finished, "I don't see how you can take the blame for what happened twenty years ago."

"No," Clint said, "actually I don't, either."

"That's good. And what about what's been happening now?"

"I might have been able to save Rose Kellogg," Clint said.

"How?"

"I don't know, but maybe I can still save her sister."

"And maybe she'll decide she still wants to kill you," Roper said. "The thing to do is to tell her who really killed her father."

"That's an interesting thought."

"What about this Wilson?" Roper asked. "Do you think he's really in love with her?"

"I don't know," Clint said. "He probably works for the banker Holmstead. We know Carver does."

"Then he'll send Carver after you," Roper said.

"Carver and some better friends than he had with him last night."

"We know where Carver lives, though, thanks to Floyd the weasel."

"We can get the jump on him."

"Yes."

"Want to do that first?"

"No," Clint said. "First I want to make sure the girl's all right, and that she's given up the notion that I killed her father."

"And the notion of killing you."

"Right."

Clint left Roper's, promising to return soon. He went to the hotel where he'd left Laura Kellogg, and hoped she was still there.

He stopped at the desk.

"Is Miss Kellogg still in her room?" he asked.

"Yes, sir," the clerk said. "I ain't seen her leave."

"Is she alone?"

"As far as I know."

"Okay, thanks."

Clint went up the stairs, but did so cautiously. Dirk Wilson might have returned and used a back door to get into the hotel.

He made his way down the hall, stopped just outside Laura's door, and listened. He couldn't hear anything, so he knocked.

There was a muffled, "Come in," from inside.

He thought about drawing his gun before entering, but that would have sent the wrong message. Instead, he simply turned the doorknob and entered the room.

Laura Kellogg was standing next to the bed, holding her rifle and pointing it right at him. Her face was expressionless.

"Well," he said, "decision time."

FORTY

When Carver entered Holmstead's office, the banker was livid.

"Do you know who was here this morning?" he demanded angrily.

"Yeah, Helen just told me."

"What do you intend to do about it?"

"I had a chance to kill Adams last night," Carver said, "and I didn't take it. You know why? Because you ain't give me the word yet!"

"Well," Holmstead said, "I'm giving you the word now. I'm not waiting to frame him anymore. I'm not waiting to play with his mind. I want him dead, and I want that girl dead."

"Both of them?"

"Both of them," Holmstead said, "today. And take Wilson with you."

"I'll need to recruit some other men."

"You recruit as many men as you want," the banker said. "I'll pay the freight, but get it done today."

"Yes, sir."

* * *

As Carver left Holmstead's office, he found Helen Kramer blocking his path.

"You can't do it, Woodrow," she said.

"I have to do it, Helen," he said, "because this is what I do."

"Woodrow, please," she said. "For me. For us."

"If I don't do this," he said, "there is no us."

"No," she said, "if you *do* it, there is no us."

He hesitated a moment, then said, "If I try to change who I am, Helen . . ."

He didn't finish. He just brushed past her and left the bank.

Holmstead left his desk and walked to the window that overlooked the street. He watched as Woodrow Carver left the building and walked down the street.

He knew he'd been too damn clever for his own good. He should have simply gotten rid of the girl when she first came to Denver. Then maybe he would not have ever had to deal with Clint Adams.

Now his only way out was to get rid of the both of them.

Laura stared at Clint for a few moments, then lowered the rifle.

"I've decided to believe you," she said.

"That's good."

"I don't know if I can forgive you, though."

"I understand."

She walked to a corner of the room and leaned the rifle against the wall.

"Did Wilson come back?" he asked.

"No," she said. "No one's been here since you left."

"Well, I found out a few things," he said.

"And will I care about what you've found out?"

"I think you will, Laura," he said, "if you want to know who really killed your father. And I mean, who actually pulled the trigger."

She turned and stared at him, her entire body tense.

"Tell me," she said. "Tell me who it was."

"Come out with me," he said. "Let's get something to eat. In fact, let's get you out of this hotel."

"What about Dirk?"

"Dirk works for a man named Holmstead," Clint said. "He's a banker. And he also employs a gunman named Woodrow Carver."

"I don't know Carver," she said, "but I know Dirk. He hasn't lied to me since I've met him."

"Well," Clint said, "we can talk about that, too. Right now come with me to get something to eat, and we'll talk about who killed your father twenty years ago."

She hesitated, then said, "All right."

She started to reach for the rifle.

"Leave the gun," he said. "We'll come back for it later."

She turned and eyed him suspiciously. He knew what she was thinking. Was he trying to get her away from her gun so he could kill her?

"Remember," he said, "you just said you decided to trust me."

"I said I decided to believe you," she corrected. "I never said I trusted you."

"Okay," he said. "For now I'll settle for you believing me. Now come on, you look like you could use a good meal."

FORTY-ONE

Hotels near the docks may have been fleabags, but restaurants within walking distance served good, hearty food, enjoyed by many of the dockworkers. Clint found one of those restaurants and ordered two steaks. Laura ate hers, and half of his.

"Haven't you been eating?" he asked.

"I haven't had much of an appetite," she said. "I don't know why today is different."

"Maybe because today you had some truth for an appetizer."

She hesitated with her last forkful in hand, then said, "Possibly," and finished it off.

"What are you going to do now?" she asked.

"I'm sure the banker will be sending someone after me," Clint said. "I'll have to take care of him."

"And what about the banker?" she asked. "What about the man who killed my father?"

"He murdered your father," Clint said. "He could still stand trial for it."

"All these years later?" she asked. "With no witnesses?"

"I'm a witness."

She remained silent.

"What do you want to do?" he asked.

"Kill him," she said. "I want to kill him."

"Is that what you really want to do, Laura?"

"Yes."

"And do you want to go back to the hotel and wait for Dirk Wilson?"

"No," she said. "I want to go back and get my things."

"Good," he said. "We can get you a room in my hotel."

"The Denver House?"

"It's very comfortable."

"I'm sure it is," she said.

"I can pay for—"

"I can afford it," she said.

"Can you?" he asked. "Where is the bulk of your money?"

"It's in . . . oh," she said. "It's in . . . that bank."

"Yes," he said. "That bank. I don't know if it's going to be accessible to you."

"It's my money," she said.

"Well," he said, "we could just go in there and ask for it."

"Do you think they'd give it to us?"

"I don't know," he said. "But it would save Holmstead the trouble of having someone look for us. This whole thing could come to a head right there in the bank, where everyone can hear what he did."

"There are still no witnesses, other than you."

"Well," Clint said, "if he tries to have us killed, that could be interpreted by some people as an admission of guilt."

"When can we go do it?" she asked.

"Anytime," he said. "Are you finished?"

"Yes," she said, "except for . . ."

"What?"

She smiled—the first real smile he'd seen from her—and said, "Dessert?"

"He wants us to what?" Dirk Wilson asked.

"To kill Adams and the girl."

"Kill Laura?" Wilson asked Carver.

"Yes. Do you have a problem with that?" he asked. "I mean, you did know that was the plan from the beginnin', right?"

"Well, yeah, but . . ."

"But what?" Carver asked. "Come on, Dirk, don't tell me she's got you twisted around her little finger."

"Of course not."

"I'll tell you what," Carver said. "I'll kill her and you take care of Adams."

"What?" Wilson didn't like the idea of going up against the Gunsmith, one-on-one, face-to-face. "I'm no quick-draw artist."

"Then the girl's yours," Carver said. "Right?"

Wilson hesitated, then said, "Right."

"I've got three more men coming," Carver said.

They were in a small run-down saloon about a block from the hotel Laura Kellogg was staying in.

"If she left with him, they'll probably go back to his hotel," Carver went on. "We can take them there."

"Her suitcase was still in the room."

He had gotten to the hotel just moments after Laura left with Clint Adams. A check of the room showed her suitcase and . . .

"Her rifle's there, too," Wilson said. "She'll be wantin' that. They'll come back there."

"Okay, then," Carver said. "We'll wait for them there. Here are the other men."

Wilson turned to see three men wearing guns enter the saloon. If they were as mean as they looked, and as good as they looked mean, then Clint Adams and the girl didn't have a chance.

FORTY-TWO

"What is it?" Laura asked when they reached the front of her hotel.

"Let's get inside."

"What's wrong?"

What was wrong was that Clint could feel in the air that something was amiss. It was confirmed when he saw how nervous the desk clerk was. The man was ready to duck down behind his desk at any moment.

"Let's get upstairs fast," he said.

They went up the stairs and hurried along the hall to her room. As soon as they entered, she grabbed her rifle.

"Your sister told me you were a crack shot," he said.

"If I was a crack shot, you'd be dead," she said. "I'm terrible."

He was hoping she'd be some help. He went to the window, stood to the side, and peered out. Sure enough, there were three men across the street, looking up at the hotel. He scanned the rooftops across the way, found one man with a rifle.

"We got company," he said.

She started for the window but he blocked the way with his arm.

"How many?"

"I see four," he said, "but I don't see Carver."

"Let me look."

"Okay, but stand to the side. There's a man on the roof across from us."

She did as she was told and looked out.

"Dirk Wilson is one of the ones across the street," she said.

"If I'm right," he said, "he'll try to talk you out by telling you they're only after me."

"If I go out there, they'll kill me, right?"

"I'm sure of it."

"Okay, then," she said. "I may not be a crack shot but I can be of some help."

"Good."

At that point a fourth man joined the three across the street.

Woodrow Carver.

"Adams!" he shouted. "Send the girl out!"

Clint reached out and slid the window open.

"I think I'll keep her in here with me, Carver."

"As a hostage?" Carver asked.

Clint didn't answer.

Clint watched as Carver moved closer to Wilson and said something. Dirk Wilson then stepped forward.

"Laura," he shouted, "if you're not bein' held against your will, come on out. You'll be safe."

Laura didn't ask Clint for permission to reply.

"I'm not coming out, Dirk. I feel safer in here."

"Laura, have I ever lied to you—"

"I'm finding out that's all you did, Dirk," she said, cutting him off. "If I come out there, I'm dead."

"Girlie," Carver said, "if you stay up there, you're dead."

"Either way, then," she said. "I still choose to stay up here."

Carver raised his arm. Clint didn't wait for it to come down.

"On the floor!" he told Laura, and they both hit the deck just as a hail of bullets flew into the room, shattering the window so that a shower of glass came down on them. Then the shooting stopped and it was silent.

"Shouldn't we shoot back?" she asked.

"Not yet," Clint said. "Let them think about it for a while."

"Can't they just wait us out?"

"Once the shooting started, there's a possibility of the law showing up," Clint said. "They're more likely to rush us."

"What do we do?"

"I'll meet them in the hallway," Clint said. "They can't fan out there."

"And what do I do?"

"Wait here in the room," he said, "in case somebody gets past me."

She peered up over the windowsill.

"I can pick the guy off the roof," she said.

"I might let you try," he said. "The other four are likely to charge us, but he might stay there and wait for a shot. Since you're not the crack shot your sister thought you were, I'd advise waiting until he stands up. And don't wait after your first shot to see if you hit him. Fire a second and a third right away."

"Got it!"

Clint peered over the sill at the four men across the street.

"They're talking it over," he said, "but they should be coming soon."

"What do we do now?" Wilson asked.

"We're goin' in," Carver said. "Sherman will stay on the roof and wait for a shot."

"Why don't we just wait them out?" Wilson asked.

"Law will be here soon," Brooks, one of the other men, said.

"Gotta get it done," the other man, Newcomb, said.

"Check your guns," Carver said. "Don't want any misfires. Once we kick in the door and get into that room, shoot anything that moves."

"Right," Brooks said.

"Woodrow . . . do we have to shoot the girl?" Wilson asked.

Carver grabbed Wilson by the front of the shirt and pulled him aside.

"You tell me right now if you can't do this, Dirk," he growled. "I ain't goin' in there with a man who ain't gonna pull his weight."

The truth was Wilson didn't want to kill Laura, but he also didn't want Carver to kill him. If he told the man he wasn't going in, that's what he thought would happen. Carver would shoot him where he stood.

"N-no, no," he said. "I can do it."

"Then no more questions," Carver said, releasing the man's shirt. "We're goin' in."

FORTY-THREE

"They're coming in," Clint said. "I'm going out into the hall to wait for them. Stay by the window, wait for your shot. Don't rush it."

"A-all right."

He stopped on his way to the door and turned.

"Laura, look at me."

She did. He knew the look in her eyes very well.

"It's okay to be scared," he said. "Don't worry about that. Just . . . don't rush."

"Okay."

He opened the door, stepped out into the hall, and closed it.

Carver, Wilson, and the other two men entered the lobby. When they did, the desk clerk dropped out of sight behind the desk.

"We're goin' up fast," Carver said. "Newcomb, you take out the door."

The large, portly man said, "Sure."

"And we go in shootin'," Carver said. "Are we ready?"

The three men all nodded.

"Okay, Newcomb, up the stairs first."

Clint heard the men come rumbling up the stairs. He drew his gun and waited.

Inside the room Laura peered over the windowsill, wishing she could just rest her rifle there and wait, but the gunman on the roof was doing that, waiting for his shot.

She had to think of a way to make him stand up.

Newcomb hit the top of the stairs first and started down the hall. Behind him Brooks and Wilson were side-by-side, with Carver taking up the rear. They all had their guns in their hands.

Clint's first shot hit Newcomb square in the chest. It stopped the big man in his tracks, then drove him back into the two men following closely behind. They both staggered, then looked shocked when they saw Clint in the hall. They brought their guns up but were too slow. Clint shot them both in the chest. He knew there was a fourth man behind them, but as they fell he heard the footsteps on the stairs again, this time rushing down.

He hurriedly opened the door and rushed back into the room.

When the shooting started in the hall, Laura decided to stand up. As she did, the man on the roof did the same thing. She remembered what Clint said. She stood her ground and took her time. The shooter on the roof didn't. He rushed his first shot and it struck the wood frame of the window. Before he could fire again, she fired very deliberately. She worked the lever and was ready to fire again, but the man had staggered back and fallen, and he wasn't getting up.

As the door opened, she turned with her rifle and Clint yelled, "It's me!"

She lowered the rifle, started to ask, "What happen—"

"Hand me your rifle," he snapped, cutting her off.

He grabbed it even before she could hand it to him, and rushed to the window. Carver was running down the street. Clint had to break out the rest of the window, sit on the windowsill, and hang out to get a bead. He sighted along the barrel and fired once. Woodrow Carver seemed to leap into the air, and when he came down it was on his stomach.

He didn't move again.

FORTY-FOUR

Clint and Laura walked into the bank, attracting the attention of all. They marched up to the teller's window—the same teller Clint had spoken with last time.

"I want to withdraw all my money," Laura said, "and close my account."

"Oh, dear," the teller said. "I'll have to get our head teller, Mr.—"

"No," Clint said, "get your bank president, Mr. Holmstead."

"Mr. Holmstead?"

"Yes," Clint said. "Get him—now!"

"Yessir."

The teller hurried away to Holmstead's office and returned with the banker in tow.

"Mr. Adams," he said, "and Miss Kellogg."

"Surprised to see us, Holmstead?" Clint asked. "Thought we'd be dead by now?"

Holmstead's eyes bounced around inside his head.

"I don't know what you mean."

"Sure you do," Clint said loudly. "You sent your pet killers after us today and failed."

"Mr. Ad—"

"They're all dead," Clint said, "and we'll be talking to the law very soon, but for now, Miss Kellogg is here for her money."

"Well, certainly," Holmstead said, "she has every right to close her account. As for the rest of it, I'm sure I don't know—"

He was cut off by a shot. It took Clint by surprise. Laura Kellogg had stepped back, raised her rifle, and shot the banker in the chest. Holmstead's eyes went wide with shock and then the life drained out of them. He crumpled to the floor. A woman started to scream. Or maybe it was a man.

"Laura—" Clint said.

"I'm sorry," she said, handing him the rifle. "I had no choice."

She turned and walked away.

Clint felt bad for both sisters. Rose had come to ask him to save Laura, and now one was dead and the other would probably end up in prison. He really hadn't done either of them any good—and he certainly was no help to their father twenty years ago.

He looked at the startled teller and said, "You better send for the police."

Watch for

BALL AND CHAIN

324th novel in the exciting GUNSMITH series
from Jove

Coming in December!

And don't miss

THE MARSHAL FROM PARIS

The Gunsmith Giant Edition 2008

Available from Jove in November!

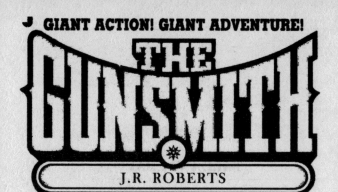

GIANT ACTION! GIANT ADVENTURE!

THE GUNSMITH

J.R. ROBERTS

penguin.com

M228AS0608

GIANT-SIZED ADVENTURE FROM
AVENGING ANGEL LONGARM.

BY TABOR EVANS

2006 Giant Edition:

LONGARM AND THE
OUTLAW EMPRESS

2007 Giant Edition:

LONGARM AND THE
GOLDEN EAGLE SHOOT-OUT

2008 Giant Edition:

LONGARM AND THE
VALLEY OF SKULLS

penguin.com